Histories and Mysteries:
Back Roads and Dangerous Curves

Reviews on Books from author Linda K. Richison

I just love a good romance novel and Linda did not let me down. Love, romance, mystery, adventure... the list goes on and on. What more could a girl ask for? Oh, spirits. Love those spirits. I have a hard time getting anything done around my home when I start reading her books. They leave you begging for more.

Sue M. Medford, Oregon

I loved the story, it kept me guessing, wondering what was around the next curve. The characters are real people, with real lives, the kind I'd like to get to know better. The fantasy elements are so plausible, I almost expected my own car to talk to me! I recommend this book to anyone looking for an escape from daily life.

Dawn K. Salem, Oregon

Loved all the books by Linda K Richison. Her characters are so relatable they feel like friends and family. Her stories immerse you in the small towns and give you such a feeling of home that you never want to leave. Once you start one of her books you are held captive by the thrills and chills that she delivers, and have to read another one as soon as you finish the first. Having to wait for the next one in the series is so hard you will find yourself reading the others again and again just to make the wait easier!

Lisa S. Salem, Oregon

All of her 5 books were so exciting to read.

I love the idea of the spirits in each book sending them on adventures.

I want to thank her so much for getting me back into reading and having some personal time to myself.

Pauline N. La Puente, California

An amazing local Author. I highly recommend her books.

Cole J. Salem, Oregon

I love that I was kept hanging on the edge. With Heart and Soul she hit a home run at the beach!

Suzie L. Aumsville, Oregon

Her books are awesome, have read them all. Normally takes me a long time to read a book, Linda's books take me a maximum of two days.

Mary O. Salem, Oregon

Histories and Mysteries: Back Roads and Dangerous Curves

Linda K. Richison

DEDICATIONS

Well, here it is, book number six. When I first started this journey eight years ago, I'd never imagined that I'd write and publish five more books. I had so many mixed feelings about releasing my first book, Heart and Souls. I wasn't sure what to expect, how people would react. Here I was about to release a part of me that was personal, fragile, and raw.

I'm so glad that I didn't let the disabling thoughts deter me from pursuing my dream. Those thoughts of uncertainty, and was-I-good-enough, that rang through my mind was a false worry. I learned that I had no cause to worry and decided not everybody was going to like them. However, I was surprised and overwhelmed at how many people did respond with positive reviews.

I'm dedicating this book to everyone that walked along beside me on this venture. I met so many people along the way, I believe, who were purposely put in my path to help make this dream come to life. As it is not possible to recognize everyone personally, I would like to thank all that offered their support, wisdom, knowledge, and who keep choosing my books. I can't express enough gratitude, and I couldn't have done it without your encouragement, kindness, and caring hearts.

TO MY READERS

Thank you for choosing my books. I invite you to step into a world of romance, mystery; laced with a touch of fantasy and scattered bits of history. The characters who are compelling, engaging, and relatable will welcome you in and pull you along in a page-turning adventure. They're sure to entertain you with their witty personalities and dazzling charm, while taking you on a journey of exposed secrets, arousing hidden clues, and then leave you hanging on a thread between fantasy and reality.

I hope you enjoy *Back Roads and Dangerous Curves*, the third book in the Histories and Mysteries series. Get ready for a windy ride on backcountry roads with Kaitlyn, Jason, and Tatiana; a baby blue T-Bird. After involving Katilyn and Jason, the spirited hotrod takes them on a dangerous mission to avenge and will stop at nothing to find and expose the man who viciously attacked and killed her years ago.

Their travels will lead you to historic Falls and picturesque landmarks in Oregon, and their story will have you clinging to your seat. To add to the mystery and mayhem, a sizzling romance unfolds, when Kaitlyn finds herself falling for the owner's son. Soon the car isn't the only thing throwing sparks and revving its engine. Fasten your seat belt put your mind on cruise control and enjoy for the ride.

Be sure to check out all of the romance, mystery, fantasy and adventure in the Histories and Mysteries series and the Spirit of Love collection.

Histories and Mysteries: Charm and Chills

Histories and Mysteries: Red Wine and Black Roses

Histories and Mysteries: Back Roads and Dangerous Curves

Spirit of Love: Heart and Souls

Spirit of Love: Lost and Found

Spirit of Love: Spice and Sassy

CONTENTS

"Find your spirit, and no challenge will keep you from
achieving your goals."

Christopher Penn

1) SUNNY

"Come on, just a little further; the pullout is just ahead ... please!" Kaitlyn pleaded to Sunny, her mechanically distressed Volkswagen bug. Her hands tightly gripped the steering wheel as she pushed forward on the wheel and then quickly back in her seat. It was a lame attempt to maneuver the vehicle off the highway safely. Hopefully, before the engine died. She heard her inner voice say, 'Baby, we can do this...!'

Five miles back, the car had started acting up. First there was a significant loss of power, next, a clunking sound, and then, to add to the orchestra of failure, black smoke billowed from the engine. This wasn't at all how she imagined her day playing out.

It had been a beautiful blue-sky day, perfect for a late spring drive in the country. She'd slipped out of work early. It wasn't like her accounting tasks needed immediate attention anyway. Capturing the moment, she'd planned her impromptu escape to Silver Falls, her little paradise. With Sunny's top-down, she'd let the wind caress her face. The air was a bit brisk, but at the same time, it was refreshing and was helping to clear her mind and reset her priorities.

"No, no, no, you can't break down here..." Kaitlyn cried out as her car exhaled the last fumes of gas and went silent. Fortunately, she'd been able to slowly guide the dying vehicle into a small pullout off the main highway, a few miles before the falls entrance.

In frustration, she rested her head on the steering wheel and gave herself a few seconds to realize her poor-me mindset wasn't going to do her any good. She called the towing company, then her dad to give him the address where he could come pick her up. After completing her calls, Kaitlyn gazed out the window and looked around at the beauty that surrounded her. Despite this minor setback, Kaitlyn wasn't going to let it spoil her day.

A smile tugged at her lips as she remembered her family's adventures in the area. After church, her mom would fix up a picnic basket. She could recall the sweet aroma of the fresh-baked apple pie and almost taste the savory morsels of the finger-licking-good fried chicken. Her dad would load up the car while she and her brother Kevin finished their chores. Within an hour, the family would be on their way. Electronics were not allowed, so for entertainment and to pass the time, their dad would tell his childhood stories repeatedly. To this day, she could recite many of them word for word. Each trip created cherished memories._Those lazy days were all about picnic lunches on grandma's handmade blanket, on a luscious green lawn, energetic frisbee fun in an open field, and nature hikes that weaved through the dense forest.

Kaitlyn pushed the past aside to take in her current surroundings. Spotting the number on the mile marker post to the left of Sunny's back bumper, caused her to shake her head in disbelief. "You've got to be kidding me," she thought upon seeing the numeral 13, right there in bold print. She'd never considered herself superstitious; however, throughout the years, that number had brought her hardship more than once. The onset of her first period had come without warning on her 13th birthday. It was not only excruciating, but it had happened at school, and it caused a horrifically embarrassing scene. When she was eighteen, the daunting 13 appeared again. Todd Nelson, the star quarterback on the football team, who wore jersey number 13, was her prom date. On the way to celebrate the special day, he accused her of cheating with his best friend Clay and left her stranded by the roadside, thirteen miles from her home. Another incident with the enemy number was on Friday the 13th, when her ex broke off their engagement. That was the worst of them all. And now, Kaitlyn had an eerie feeling that this sign could be related to the rest.

She scanned the open forest and watched as a wild bunny scurried off the gravel road onto a narrow trail. Under other circumstances, Kaitlyn would've followed the cute white-tailed creature into the woods. She wondered where the trail ended, and she made a mental note to come back and check it out another time.

The sound of a car passing by on the main road caused Kaitlyn to turn around. She usually considered the falls highway to be safe, but suddenly an eerie sensation rushed through her veins and struck her in the gut. The uninvited emotion was scary and left her feeling exposed and vulnerable, sitting alone in the desolate pullout. As she embraced herself to ward off the spine-tingling chill, she looked out into the woods and wondered what faceless evil might be out there. After shaking off the weird sensation, the trembling subsided. Kaitlyn looked for a distraction, perhaps a game app on her phone, to concentrate on until the tow truck showed up. She hoped it would be soon.

Fortunately, it wasn't long before the tow truck came to her rescue and she was parked in the towing yard, twenty minutes later.

"Seriously, are you sure?" Kaitlyn whined to Bill, the small town's only mechanic who'd diagnosed her Volkswagen bug. Feeling distraught, she was trying to digest the bad news.

"I'm sorry, Kaitlyn," the man in blue oil-stained coveralls replied with sympathy. "It looks like your baby has seen better days. She's got a cracked radiator, and her engine is shot."

"Great!" Kaitlyn said, letting out a frustrated moan. "What am I supposed to do with Sunny now?" She looked to Bill for answers.

"Why don't I see if I can find the parts so we can get you and 'Sunny' back on the road?" Bill suggested with a smile.

Kaitlyn went over to her wounded road companion, leaned up against Sunny's fender, and raked her hands through her short and sassy red hair. "You know, this car has been by my side for over fifteen years. I'd hate to give up on her," she said, patting the hood of her broken baby.

"I understand completely," Bill commented, attempting to wipe the oil off his hands, with little luck. "In my younger years, I had a red 1950 Ford pickup. I bought it from the original owner in mint condition. It saw me through many after-party drives of shame, rumbled through town when pulling cans on my wedding day, and helped my three boys learn how to drive on the back roads," he said, thinking back.

"So, what happened to it?"

"She still runs like a dream, and when I get the urge, I take her out for a spin. So, what do you want to do with Sunny?" he asked, wiping a bead of sweat from his brow.

She looked up at Bill and shielded her eyes with her hand from the blinding sunlight. "Only one thing to do, fix her," Kaitlyn replied with a hopeful face. She ran her hand along the side of the car. "You're going to be ok, baby." She wished the car could connect with her, but she knew that was never going to happen, an impossible request for sure.

"Why don't we go into the office and discuss your options? I'll get you a business card. You can call me later with your decision," Bill said, heading to a small building and opening the door. "I warn you it's a bit messy; the maid hasn't been in."

Kaitlyn stepped into the cramped quarters, which were no bigger than her parent's master bedroom. She thought messy was an understatement; the place was a disaster.

Bill moved some boxes from a small sofa and invited her to sit.

Noticing the stains on the excessively worn piece of furniture, Kaitlyn politely declined.

"It should only take me a couple of minutes to find a business card," he announced, walking behind a counter.

More like an hour, she thought as she stared at the cluttered space piled high with magazines, small car parts, and fast-food restaurant bags.

"I know it's here somewhere," he laughed, stirring up the settled dust.

The dust particles flew into the air, and Kaitlyn had to rub her nose to ward off a sneeze while she perused the man cave. The pale walls needed dire attention. Fortunately, miscellaneous objects covered most of the wall space.

"I can't understand it. My stack of business cards was right under this pile yesterday," Bill said in frustration. He took off his ball cap, raked his hands through his wavy hair, and replaced it on his head. "Of course, there has been more junk added to this pile in the last twenty-four hours. Sorry it's taking so long. Please help yourself to some coffee or water," he offered, pointing to the corner.

One look at the outdated, brown stained coffee machine, and Kaitlyn squinched her nose and put on a fake smile. "You know, I've been drinking too much coffee lately. Water works," she politely commented, removing a bottle of spring water from the small refrigerator.

Bill looked up and caught the attempt at a disguised look of disgust on her face. He shook his head. How had his office become a hoarder's office in the making?
It needed a good cleaning and could use some organization. "Hey, would you by chance know of anyone who would want a part-time job as my assistant? As you can see, I could use some help to get this place in order, it seems to have taken on a life of its own," Bill smirked. "I need someone to answer the phones, make appointments, light bookkeeping, and keep me on track."

"They could tidy it up, as long as they limited the woman touches. No offense, but mostly guys come in here. They could buy what they need. I'll give them a budget to work with, and we can negotiate the pay."

Kaitlyn pondered his offer as she took a closer look at the chaotic mess. Her part-time job got her by, but she could use the extra money to pay off her student loans, and now, Sunny's repair costs. She tried to imagine a clean and organized counter, a small desk behind it. Maybe a leather sofa on a braided rug, and car magazines on top of a corner table to update the small waiting area, and a new coffee machine, one that didn't scare off the customers. Of course, the walls would need to be painted, but most of the wall art could remain. She could live with the sleek, black Lamborghini poster, stark yellow Pennzoil poster, and the pegboard loaded with business cards, but they might have to negotiate an alternative for the torn and faded centerfold of the half-naked woman in a skimpy red bikini.

With the new design in mind, it might be doable, she thought, considering the idea. "I suppose I could think about doing it," Kaitlyn said, gritting her teeth and hoping it wasn't a big mistake.

"Really?" Bill asked. "That would be great. When can you start?"

His comment startled her. She wasn't expecting to decide tonight. "Wow, that's a little fast; I am barely in the decision phase. Let me think about it, and I'll come by on Monday and we can discuss it in more detail. Here, let me help you find the cards." Then, as she moved a pile of magazines, Kaitlyn uncovered the box of business cards and an entrancing flyer that captivated her attention.

She instantly fell in love with the cherry '55 T-bird in the photo. Lit up like a piece of art on wheels, painted in original thunderbird blue, strutting a smooth, youthful body, it got her heart racing. She wet her lips as she imagined trailing her fingers down the sleek fiberglass rakish long hood. Her Uncle Jack had one almost identical to this car. He called it the second love of his life, and the first time she rode in the car, Kaitlyn quickly understood why. It was her first exposure to the world of classic cars. It was also that luxurious two-seat roadster that sparked her passion for beautiful vehicles. Kaitlyn's excitement elevated when she noticed the for-sale sign resting on the windshield. "Please tell me this car is still for sale," she said, biting her lip and sending Bill a hopeful look.

"She was as of last night," Bill replied. "That's Tatiana. She used to belong to my brother-in-law Greg," he commented as he looked away. "He took her out for a drive, as he usually did on Sundays, and when he didn't return that night, his wife Sara reported him missing. The car was found days later, but Greg wasn't anywhere around." Bill looked up and casually brushed a tear from his eye and continued. "After searching the surrounding area for weeks with no clues, the authorities called off the search. Next week, on May 7th, it will be two years. I can't believe it's been that long. I sure miss my good friend."

"I'm so sorry," Kaitlyn said, offering sympathy.

"Thank you. It's my sister Sara and her son Jason that are suffering the most. She is still grieving and confused over the incident, and Jason is angry and carries a chip on his shoulder. It's so hard for them, especially when they've had no closure," he admitted, shaking his head. "She just gave me that flyer yesterday, told me the car reminded her too much of Greg, and someone else should have the opportunity to own the sweet lady."

"I'd love to see it," Kaitlyn said as the picture of the car pulled her further in. It took her by surprise as she saw herself seated in the driver's seat in the photograph. The vision came alive. With the car top down, she could feel the warmth of the sun on her shoulders and the wind as it lifted her hair. She did a double-take and rubbed her eyes, then took another look, and everything was back to normal. For the second time today something had spooked her, and she didn't like the unsettling feeling.

Seeing the furrowed look on Kaitlyn's face, Bill questioned her condition. "Is everything ok?"

"Uh... yes. It's been a long day, and with the stress of everything that has happened, I'm feeling a little tired."

"If you like, I can call my sister later today and let her know you're interested in looking at the car."

"I'd appreciate that," she replied, placing the flyer back on the pile.

"Now, Kaitlyn, have you made up your mind about Sunny, or do you want to call me later with your answer?" he asked.

Kaitlyn shrugged, "I guess you can start looking for the parts. We are in it for life," she said with a slight laugh.

"I'll check around tomorrow. Hopefully, I can locate a used engine."

"Sounds great," Kaitlyn replied as her eyes wandered back to the picture.

"Do you need a ride? I'll be done in an hour and can take you home."

"Thanks, but I called my dad earlier, and he should be waiting outside or almost here. Please let me know what you find out from your sister."

"Here, why don't you take Tatiana with you?" he asked, handing her the flyer and business card. "Tell your dad I said hi." Then his phone rang, which ended their conversation, and Bill waved to Kaitlyn as he tended to the next customer.

Kaitlyn stood outside and let the sun rays caress her face while she waited for her dad. Her eyes were glued to the flyer when he pulled up. "Thanks for the rescue," she said while climbing into the car.

"What, you expect me to leave my favorite daughter stranded?" her dad Rob teased.

Kaitlyn tilted her head. "You only have one daughter. You could, however, say I was your favorite child."

"Hmm..." Rob replied. "I'm not sure how Seth would like that."

"He's just a brother. Come on, dad, admit it, I'm much better than him," she laughed. "Why are you driving mom's SUV?"

"I brought it into town to be serviced. There are too many gadgets and buttons in these new models. I know enough to operate this vehicle, but that's about it. It reminds me of the spaceship model I sat in at the state fair as a child." He laughed.

"I know, right, way too techy." When it came to cars, she was more like her dad. Give her a classic car any day. Besides the basics, all she needed was a working heater and air conditioning, if she was lucky. However, a quality radio and speakers were a must.

"Be careful what you touch, don't want to blast to the moon," he snickered. "So, what happened to Sunny?"

"She has a cracked block, and the radiator is shot. Bill is looking for used parts. He also says Hi. I don't understand. She was running fine yesterday. I didn't even get a sign," Kaitlyn said with a pout.

"That happens, especially with older cars. Sunny has been a dependable ride for many years. It was only a matter of time before she'd need a major repair. Are you going to ask Seth to put the engine in?"

"No, Bill is handling it. Seth is too busy and doesn't have enough time with his family as it is. I may have an idea for a temporary replacement, though," Kaitlyn expressed, bursting with excitement.

"I don't think I'm going to like this," Rob expressed, knowing his daughter's impulsive nature always led to trouble.

Kaitlyn turned to face her dad and showed him the flyer. "I want her."

"I see," Rob said, briefly glancing at the flyer. "Very nice, but what about Sunny?" he asked, returning his eyes to the road.

"Well, I can't get rid of her, and I think it's about time to get her a sister," she said to win over her dad. "Isn't she a beauty?" she asked, sending him dreamy eyes.

"Yes, but your mom has made it clear; we are not to bring any more vehicles onto the property," he reminded his daughter.

"No problem, I'll keep it at my house," Kaitlyn said, solving the issue. "The land is mine, and she rarely comes down to visit," she said, pushing her point.

Her parents owned a ranch house in the country on twenty-five acres. As a college graduation present, they gave her and Seth an acre of land on opposite ends of the property. She lived in a cute tiny house designed and built for her simple lifestyle. Seth, his beautiful wife Jena, and their adorable five-year-old son Carson lived in a mobile home while their custom home was in the process of being built. The arrangement seemed to work for the family. Her mom got to be close to her children and grandchildren but wasn't always in their family affairs.

"You know you can't hide anything from your mom. But let's not get ahead of ourselves. You might decide you don't want the car. The three of us will drive out there and check it out."

"Three?" Kaitlyn said with a questioning look.

"Yes, I'd like Seth to tag along. We are a team. I work on the body and interior, and his specialty is under the hood. I wouldn't feel confident giving you an honest review."

"I don't want him to go," Kaitlyn said, pouting. "He'll try and take her."

Rob shook his head. "When are you going to get past that?"

"When he stops stealing my cars," she said with a snarl.

"Kaitlyn dear, that only happened once. If I remember correctly, your brother got stuck with a lemon that needed extensive work," Rob said, reminding his daughter of the outcome of the incident.

"Yes, but he went behind my back and bought it when he knew I had my heart set on it. I'm afraid he'll do the same with this one," Kaitlyn said with a sigh.

"I don't think you have to worry about that, pretty sure he learned his lesson," he said, turning into their driveway.

Kaitlyn gazed out the window. The road was bordered on each side by a wood fence and rows of perfectly manicured fir trees. At night, the twinkling lights wrapped around the posts reminded her of something magical. When she was young, Kaitlyn pretended the car was a carriage, and it was taking her to an enchanted kingdom, where a handsome prince waited to kiss her.

"You want me to drop you off at your place, or are you coming up to the house?" Rob asked when he came to a stop at a gravel intersection.

"Home, please. I've been gone longer than I had expected and I'm sure Gina misses me." Gina was her two-year-old mini-Australian Husky and best friend. Gina's mom had decided to give birth under the porch at her parents' house. Kaitlyn had volunteered to crawl under the porch to retrieve the puppies. After handing four puppies to

Seth, she picked up the fifth, a marble-colored, playful pup. One look into her unique eyes, one green and the other blue, and Kaitlyn fell instantly in love. Her brother had chosen the only male, a wobbly, black-coated heart-grabber that walked immediately into his heart with his furry white socks. He named his new friend Braxton. They pleaded with their parents to keep them all, but eventually they sold the rest to good homes.

When the car stopped, Kaitlyn placed a kiss on her dad's cheek. "Thanks for the ride. I'll call when I hear back from Bill. Meanwhile, you can think of a story to tell mom," she giggled as she exited the car.

"You are rotten sometimes," he said with a smirk.

"Yes, but you love me anyway," she replied with a sassy attitude.

Gina was waiting at the gate. Her stubby tail excitedly wagged when Kaitlyn opened it. "Hey girl," she said, squatting to greet her loving pup. Satisfied with her cuddles and usual belly rub, Gina fetched a ball, hinting it was time to play.

After tossing the ball until her arm hurt, Kaitlyn called to Gina, "Let's go in, girl." Still wanting more playtime and under protest, the disappointed dog gave in and followed her owner through the open glass-paned doors. Kaitlyn took the flyer from her purse and placed her bag on an antique table near the door. She then put her shoes neatly under the inside step. Kaitlyn had learned early on that living in a tiny house was all about organization. Everything had a place, and if she weren't consistent, her place would get out of control.

Kaitlyn loved her little home, as it was cozy and quaint, and living in the small quarters had taught her that less is more. The design was based on tiny-house dimensions and layouts. Her major request was to have storage units inserted in every available space. The high vaulted ceilings were one of her favorite features. It gave the illusion of a larger area, and the open wall-length blinded windows brought in the natural light.

She grabbed a soda from her fridge and with the flyer in her hand, turned on her tunes, plopped down on her sectional black leather sofa, and removed a blanket from one of the modular lift-up storage compartments. Snuggled up with Gina, she took a sip from her can and gazed out the big bay window. The eastern ridge with the layered slopes of water-colored landscape, and Douglas firs adorning the rolling hills, painted a spectacular view. In her opinion, this was the best piece of land on the entire property.

Kaitlyn stared at the car on the flyer. "Isn't she awesome?" she asked her curious fur-baby. "I don't know what it is about this car, but something is drawing me to her." Running her fingers over the outline, Kaitlyn could almost feel the cold steel steering wheel in her hands.

Her content mood was interrupted when a familiar song, connected with a sad relationship memory, started playing on the radio. Kaitlyn stared at a photograph on the wall of Bryan, her ex, and herself. Wrapped in love by the heart-shaped frame, their smiles showed all the good times they'd had together. All their memories were still fresh in her fragile thoughts. She couldn't bear to say good-bye to the picture of them together at the beach, even though it didn't seem to be a problem for him. The couple in the photo was a reminder that true love doesn't exist, at least not in her world. Not wanting to drive down break-up lane, Kaitlyn turned the dial to her favorite reggae station and started dancing around her small living room. With every move, she shook off a piece of her hurtful past. Gina barked at the energy and ran in circles, joining in on the dance party.

After eating a tuna salad for a late lunch, Kaitlyn checked her emails and social groups and handled some mundane chores. Being patient was never her strong suit, mostly when there was a beautiful car involved. She had even tried to mind-will her phone to ring—very drastic measures.

Just when she thought her patience had finally run out, Kaitlyn got the call. It had only been a couple of hours since she'd talked to Bill at the shop, but to her, it seemed like an eternity. "Hello," she answered, trying not to seem eager.

"Hi Kaitlyn, Bill here. I talked to my sister, and I have good news. The car is still available, and you're welcome to come over and check it out. She just needs advance notice."

"Awesome, how about tonight, say around 6:00?" Kaitlyn replied, not able to contain her excitement.

Bill chuckled. "I'll call her and see what I can do. If you don't hear back from me in the next fifteen minutes, then it's a go."

"Ok," Kaitlyn said, then ended the call. Those minutes were going to seem like another eternity, she thought, playing the waiting game again.

At 5:45, Kaitlyn sat in the passenger seat in her dad's sky-blue Chevy Silverado, 4 by 4. Her brother, who they'd picked up at his store, was sitting in the backseat of the extended cab, talking about his day at work, trying hard to get his digs in. "It was awful nice of you to ride out with me to check out my car," he teased.

"You stay away from it," she warned. "It's not your car. If it were up to me, you wouldn't even be here. Dad seems to think we could use your expert opinion on her insides."

"Ouch," Seth said, pretending to be hurt. Then he laughed and gently tapped Kaitlyn on the shoulder. "Little Sis, I swear to you I'm not after your car. How many times do I have to apologize? It was a big misunderstanding."

"Ooh what's that awful smell? Did you step in something?" Kaitlyn asked, plugging her nose.

"Well, I would've gone home and changed, but someone was so obsessed with a car, I didn't have time to."

"It's so gross, can't we toss your work boots in the back of truck?" she asked, rolling down the window, over-dramatizing her actions as she gasped for air.

"I have a better idea, why don't we toss you in the back of the truck," he sarcastically replied.

"Hey, you two," Rob called out to get their attention. "Sounds like I'm riding with young, immature children instead of two grown adults. Can't we discuss something else less threatening to either of you?"

Sensing their dad's agitation with their bickering, they cooled their quarreling and turned their conversion into easy surface topics, like work, weather, and family.

Her dad informed them that their mother had gone out with friends after work, so this time they were in the clear. He stressed that he was still apprehensive about going against her wishes by bringing another car onto the property. And in his opinion, hiding it wasn't a smart solution,

Kaitlyn told him she'd take the rap, and in this case, it was better to ask for forgiveness than permission.

Rob pulled into a private drive that led them to a large farmhouse. A tall woman with shoulder-length highlighted blond hair, dressed in jeans and a sweatshirt, navigated them to a big red barn. Kaitlyn was enamored by how the grieving lady carried herself, proud in her long strides in a pair of tattered cowboy boots. Kaitlyn wondered if the poised lady wore the Stetson, slanted down on her left side, to hide her sad eyes.

The woman greeted them with a brief introduction in front of a large barn door.

"Hi, I'm Sara, and my son Jason is supposed to be here shortly. You must be Kaitlyn. I hear you're interested in looking at Tatiana. She was the pride of his eye," Sara said, turning to hide her sadness. "I just want her to go to a good home." With that, she pulled back the door, and there stood the most beautiful thing Kaitlyn had ever seen.

"Oh my," Kaitlyn gasped, bringing her hand up to her mouth. "The picture doesn't do her justice." Then a strange feeling drew her closer to the car. She reached out and touched the hood. She expected to feel cool metal on her fingers. Instead, a surge of burning heat crawled up her arm, which startled Kaitlyn, and she quickly removed her still-tingling hand. She hid her confusion, deciding it had to be her imagination. She placed her hand on it again. This time it was ice cold. Kaitlyn pulled at her hand, almost frozen to the piece, and rubbed her hands together to warm them. What happened, she wondered. She was relieved no one had witnessed the scene. What had caused the drastic temperature switch? Even though she was freaked out and wanted answers, she didn't want to take the chance of mentioning it and sounding crazy. So instead, Kaitlyn pushed it to the back of her mind and turned to her dad. "What do you think of her?"

"She sure is something special," her dad agreed as he walked around inspecting the body.

"Wow, little sis, this is a lot of car!" Seth expressed as he sat in the driver's seat.

"Yes, it is," commented a young man who'd just joined the group.

"This is my son Jason," Sara said with a loving smile. "He's here to answer any questions. I love riding in her, but I wouldn't be of any help with any mechanical questions."

Jason walked past Kaitlyn, oblivious to her existence, and stuck his head in the car. "So, are you familiar with classic cars?"

"Yes, my sister and I grew up around them. She sure is hot," Seth answered, touching every knob.

"I have the keys if you'd like to take her for a spin," Jason said, directing his attention to Seth.

"Excuse me!" Kaitlyn commented, not at all impressed with the arrogant man. She studied the tall and stocky jerk and then mentally added him to her jerk list. "I'm the ONE interested in buying this car."

Jason raised his head, and with a smug look, he laughed. "You? This car is way too much for a girl to handle."

"A girl?" Kaitlyn said, seeing red, her anger flaring. This guy didn't know who he was dealing with, and she planned on letting him know. "How about you give me the keys? I promise I'll be gentle," she said, snidely shooting imaginary eye daggers at him. Then she moved him to the top of the jerk list.

2) THE UNEXPECTED GUEST

It was apparent by the expression on everyone's faces that Kaitlyn's remark had made an impact. Rob rolled his eyes and commented under his breath, "Kaitlyn, no!" However, he was aware that his subliminal message probably wouldn't break through her strong will and determination.

Sara hid a humorous smile. She was entertained by this young lady challenging her son and was interested in how it would all play out.

Jason turned his attention back to Seth with a questionable look etched on his face. "Is she for real?" he asked, staring at the cute, sassy lady through the windshield.

"Very," Seth confirmed with a smirk.

"Should I be concerned?" he asked.

"I assume that since you have to ask, you don't have a sister and have never been married," Seth said, checking out the inside of the car.

"That is correct. But how did you know?" Jason asked, relieved there was a glass barrier to ward off her imaginary eye daggers.

"Oh, I have my ways. Good luck," Seth said with a devious grin pointing to Kaitlyn as she approached the car.

"Hi, I'm Kaitlyn. I'd love to have the keys so I can drive MY car," she said with a fake smile. Then she held out her hand.

Jason squeezed the keys in his hand. "Ahh... come to think of it, I might've spoken too soon. We aren't even sure what condition it's in. It probably doesn't even run."

"Jason!" his mom scolded. "You know very well it runs. Your dad took better care of that car than any of our other vehicles." She sighed, looking at her guests. "He was always talking to it," Sara admitted, shaking her head. "I assure you the car is in excellent condition. My brother gave her a thorough inspection last week, and said she was ready to go." With a stern look Sara turned to face her son. "Jason, now please show some manners, which I know you have, and give Kaitlyn the keys."

"Yes, show me some manners!" Kaitlyn repeated in a snarky tone. She was getting tired of this man's childish behavior and snobby attitude.

Jason looked at his mom as he flipped the keys around in his hand. "Mom, what would dad think if we sold this car to some girl whom we hardly know?"

Kaitlyn raised her hand. "Can I please say something?"

"Nothing has stopped you yet," Jason answered in a condescending tone.

Kaitlyn rolled her eyes and dismissed his comment. "I don't have to prove anything to you or plead my case. It's not like I'm adopting a child or anything like that, sheesh," she said, shaking her head. "Classic cars have been in my family since before I was born. My mom came close to giving birth to me in Betsy, my grandma's Studebaker. My brother Seth," she pointed to him sitting in the driver's seat, "is a wiz under the hood, and my dad Rob, standing next to your mother, does the best bodywork and detailing in town. So, I promise she'll be in good hands."

Jason dropped his head, a look of defeat plaguing him. Kaitlyn watched as he walked over to his mom and confronted her. His brown eyes turned sad and hollow. "Mom, how can you sell her? What if, by some miracle, dad comes home? Can you live with that?" he posed a painful question.

Sara stepped close to her son and put her arm around his shoulders, drawing him close as though he was a little child once again. "We agreed it would be the best thing to do. It's about time for both of us to move on," she said, brushing his blond curls from his eyes.

Jason abruptly pulled away; his sadness now masked in anger. "I've changed my mind. Maybe you can sell his car, get rid of his belongings, and pretend he no longer exists, but I can't. Sorry, I will have no part in this," he informed her. He then threw the keys on the ground and stormed off.

Sara stood frozen, her face full of shock and pain. After she shook off the moment, she picked up the keys and handed them to Kaitlyn. "I'm sorry you all had to witness our family drama. It's been two years since Greg's disappearance, but sometimes the feeling is still as raw and fragile as though it was yesterday. My son is still hurting. Please excuse his mood. I'm sure when his head has cleared, he'll be able to think more rationally."

"Maybe it would be better if we come back at another time," Kaitlyn suggested, refusing to take the keys. She motioned Seth out of the car.

"Would you mind? I can call you later," Sara offered.

"Not at all," Rob answered. "You know, kids are quite resilient. He'll come around and bounce back."

"We can only hope. Jason's father was his life. He misses him so much," Sara said, following the deep impression in the mud left by her confused and heartbroken son.

"Thank you for taking the time to see us tonight," Rob commented as they loaded into his truck.

"Glad you could make it out," she said, then closed the barn door.

An eerie silence joined the trio on their ride home. Kaitlyn could tell the incident had touched them all. Her happy bubble had burst, and sadness filled her.

"Well, one good thing, we don't have to make up a story to tell your mom," Rob said to lighten the mood.

"Sorry, Sis. I know how much this car meant to you," Seth commented, also trying to console his sister.

"Thank you, Seth. I appreciate your sentiment. That car means more to Jason than he realizes. He's not ready to give it up. Taking that car would be like stealing a part of his dad. I couldn't do it." Kaitlyn's heart softened for the young and troubled man and moved him completely off the Jerk list.

"Well, there's always Betsy," Seth teased.

"Fine with me. Dad can you please drop me off at the lower garage? Looks like I'm in for some Kaitlyn and Betsy bonding time," she said with a giggle.

"Gotcha," he said, shooting his daughter a wink.

After Kaitlyn said her goodbyes, she climbed into the bright green 1948 Studebaker and turned the key. The one thing that set this car apart from most was that it contained a touch starter hidden under the floor's clutch. She had to press her foot clear to the floorboard to start it. She loved the rumble of the engine and the musty smell. It reminded her of her grandmother and all the loving memories they'd shared riding together. For the most part, it was in good condition. Her dad had recovered the seats in light tan, and the large four-door vehicle had all the functional components necessary to make it a safe and dependable ride. "Hey girl it's just me and you for a while," she said with a smile, patting the dusty dash. "If only you could talk, I bet you have some incredible stories to share."

Kaitlyn awoke the next morning with a cold nose on her cheek. "Good morning Gina," she said, half grinning at her baby. Her eyes squinted while glancing at the time. "Baby, it's only 7:00 AM, and it's Saturday," she said, closing her eyes. However, Gina didn't care what time or which day it was as she nudged Kaitlyn's arm. "Ok, ok," she said to the excited pup who was dancing in circles. Slowly she dragged herself out of bed and put on her robe and slippers.

After she opened the door to let Gina out, Kaitlyn filled her fur baby's food dish and brewed herself a cup of coffee. Today the sky was clear, so she bundled up in a heavy down jacket, and took the hot coffee outside to the front patio to embrace the birth of the new day. She sat on the outside sofa, wrapped her hands around the warm ceramic cup, and let the morning wash over her. Kaitlyn took a deep breath cleansing her body with the air; brisk, fresh, and not yet tainted with pollutant toxins. The sun, peeking over the horizon, colored the sky with beautiful hues of a fiery glow that brought more than just light to her day. Each morning offered a slightly different picture, just like her variety filled life.

The sound of her phone pulled her from this meditative state. The number and ring tone were unfamiliar, which led her to believe it was a scam call. Who else would be calling before nine? Most of her friends were still in bed, heads buried in blankets, hungover from a late Friday night of clubbing. She usually didn't answer an unknown number, but something compelled her to make an exception.

"Hello," Kaitlyn greeted the caller.

'Hi. Is this Kaitlyn? This is Jason. We met under some unfavorable circumstances yesterday."

She was shocked that he had called her. "Yes, this is. What's up?" she asked, playing it casually.

"I wanted to apologize for my actions yesterday. They were inexcusable," Jason confessed.

"No worries. I can't imagine losing my dad," she said, offering comfort.

"Well, I acted like a jerk, and I'd like to make it up to you."

"That's ok, we're good. But thanks anyway."

"Please, I insist. If you are still interested in seeing the car, I could meet you somewhere. You name the time and place."

"That's really not necessary," Kaitlyn replied, even though the offer was tempting.

"I won't take no for an answer," Jason pleaded.

"Hmm," Kaitlyn mumbled, mulling over the idea. "Well, if it's not an imposition, I guess we can meet. How about the Coffee House in Stayton, say around 4:00 PM today? I'll be the one in the bright green Studebaker."

"Great," he said. "I'll see you then. Bye, and you're welcome."

"For what?" Kaitlyn asked to the silence. "What did he mean by that?" she wondered, grasping the coffee cup tighter.

It was obvious to her that this guy was still working on some emotional issues. She didn't want to be there if he had another breakdown. Maybe in a public place he would be able to stay in control. She decided to continue with the plan, especially since she'd get a chance to drive Tatiana. Hopefully, he would give up the keys this time, she thought, excitement cooking inside her. Well, there were several hours between now and four. If she was going to make it to Saturday morning family brunch at her parents, a shower was her next destination.

Forty-five minutes later, Kaitlyn was dressed and checking out her reflection in the full-length mirror. She had chosen straight-legged jeans, an oversized blue sweater she let drape over her shoulder, and a pair of one-inch tan wedges that completed the look. Her finger styled short hair was held together with mousse and moveable hairspray. Her hairdresser called it bold and sassy. It worked for her oval face, was a natural doo, and fit her low maintenance life. It wasn't her nature to make a fuss over makeup and hair, however she treated herself to a monthly manicure and pedicure. Today Kaitlyn added a touch a makeup, telling herself it wasn't because of her 4:00 meeting that afternoon with Jason. She was only interested in the car.

"Come, Gina, let's go up to the house. Braxton will be there," she said, calling to the dog. "It's such a beautiful day. Let's hike it, girl."

Kaitlyn approached her family home. Her parents had it built soon after they were married. It was designed to embrace the farm-house style to satisfy their needs and wants and included a large wraparound front porch.

She could remember the grueling hours painting alongside her brother and dad last year as they updated the outside.

The inside also held to the farm-house flair. The integrated antiques and a few contemporary pieces kept the homey feel. It was simple as well as warm and welcoming. It showed love and provided comfort.

Kaitlyn walked up to the house and opened the white picket fence. It was built originally as a welcome but now protected her mom's precious Pomeranians, Jack and Angel, and her grandson, from roaming the property. Kaitlyn envied her mother's green thumb and admired her ability to create a landscaped masterpiece. Their yard looked like a picture out of a garden magazine, from the perfectly manicured luscious green grass to the flourishing plants and hanging baskets full of beautiful flowers.

Everything came together to create an invitation to a loving home.

The yard art, a mixture of garage sale treasures and great store buys, gave the area character and style.

Not to say her yard wasn't lovely. It was simple and still fit her low-maintenance lifestyle.

Kaitlyn followed the unique steppingstones, capturing specific family events. The first stone had an imprint of two doves and the date of her parent's marriage. The next two stones recognized her and Seth, each containing their birthdate and their baby hand and footprints. The next one gave tribute to Seth and Jena's wedding day. Following theirs was the birthday stone for Seth's son, Carson. Kaitlyn breathed a heavy sigh and squatted by the last one. She brushed off the leaves with her hand. It was bare and was waiting for her family. That would be a while, she thought, as her heart was on a hiatus and wasn't interested in falling or enduring another painful break-up anytime soon.

At the top of the porch, Kaitlyn stood on the large deck. As always, it was ready for company or perfect for a daytime nap on the porch swing or a romantic night of stargazing, snuggled in the wicker sofa. She could recall many nights cuddled next to Bryan, discussing, and imagining their future together. Kaitlyn wiped the sad memory from her mind, then opened the screen door and braced herself for the welcoming chaos sure to be lurking behind it.

As the door came open, so did the chatter of voices from the dining area. Braxton instantly spotted his sister, and the chasing game erupted in the foyer. Then, the Pomeranians joined in the fun, and it was trouble times four. "Auntie Kate," Carson screamed as he made a running beeline to Kaitlyn. His hand was holding onto his droopy drawers, and his curly hair was covering his eyes.

"My favorite little guy," Kaitlyn said as she picked up her adorable nephew and hugged him.

"Where's your belt?" she asked, knowing he'd taken off because he didn't like it. Then she set him back on the floor.

"I don't know!" he answered with little concern.

Kaitlyn smiled and brushed his hair to the side and whispered in his ear, "I'll tell you a secret. I don't like them either."

"You don't?" Carson asked interestedly.

"But one day when I was your age, my pants came down, and everyone could see my undies. I tell you; it was very embarrassing. You don't want that to happen to you? Do you?"

"No way," Carson said with an alarming look.

"So, let's go find it," she said, taking his hand.

"Later," he replied, already dismissing the task. His short-attention-span kept him moving. "Grandma made a special pancake for me to decorate. Come sit by me," he said, pulling her along. "There's chocolate chips and other yummy toppings."

"We'd better hurry before daddy eats it," Kaitlyn said, causing them both to giggle.

Most of the family was all gathered around the dining room table. Her mom's favorite china dressed it up for the occasion.

The aroma of bacon and pancakes sweetened the air as everyone took their seats. Her mom always went all out and usually ended up cooking enough food for the entire county. The brunch was a family affair, with others helping to prepare the meal.

"Mommy!" Carson screamed, running to his mother, who was untying her apron string. "Auntie Kate is going to help me decorate my pancake. Make sure she sits by me," he sweetly demanded.

"That's great," Jena said as she bent down and caught the little boy in her arms. "You'd better go save a seat." Then she let go of the squirming little boy, his legs moving before they hit the floor.

"Hey Jena," Kaitlyn said, hugging her sister-in-law.

"Hi, Sis," Jena said, hugging her back. "I swear I get more flour on me than what ends up in the bowl," she said, brushing a white spot off her jeans. Then she removed a hair clip to free her long brown hair.

Kaitlyn smiled and turned her attention to the table. She smiled at the bouquet of yellow apology roses on the table and wondered what her dad had done this time. Before taking her seat, she kissed her mom on the cheek, and the scent of maple and floral perfume tickled her nose. As always, her mom Karen was dressed up for the occasion. Her blond mid-length hair was pulled back in a clip, and peach color brightened her lips. There wasn't a dress code. It was merely come as you are. Most of them did and were usually casual in jeans. However, her mom never passed up an opportunity to dress up. "You look beautiful as always."

"Thank you, honey," she said humbly and waited for Kaitlyn to sit before calling the group to attention. "Good morning, as always, it warms my heart to have the family together. Let's all hold hands and give thanks. God bless this family, this food, and this life." Amen echoed through the room, which gave the signal to dig in.

They passed around trays of food. Choices of drinks, including mimosas, were selected. The sounds of clinking silver and happy voices exploded throughout the room.

"Looks like we are going to have an addition to the family," Karen announced with a grin.

Kaitlyn's eyes lit up as she pointed to her brother and sister-in-law, "Another baby?"

"No!" was firmly replied by both parties.

"I don't understand. Is one of the animals pregnant?" Kaitlyn asked, now growing curious.

"Seems like you have a secret admirer that leaves interesting gifts," Jena smirked.

Kaitlyn gave a deep sigh. "You guys. What gives?" she asked, dumbfounded.

"Those roses on the table are for you," her mom said with a wide grin. "I'm not sure what you did, but a handsome young man dropped them off this morning, along with a beautiful blue T-Bird, which is parked at the upper garage."

"What?" Kaitlyn shrieked. "Jason was here this morning?" Then his words, "You are welcome," repeated in her mind.

"What did I tell you all about bringing another car onto the property? Soon it's going to look like a car lot," Karen scolded.

Kaitlyn looked at her dad, her eyes pleaded for salvation, but as he purposely looked away, she knew that he wasn't going to be any help. "Mom, my mind isn't fully made up yet. However, if I do decide to take the car, I promise to keep it at my house."

"What are you going to do with Sunny?" she asked before taking a bite of her bacon.

Kaitlyn shrugged, "I'm going to keep her, and I think she needs a sister."

"Hmm," Karen said, tapping her nails on the table. "We're expecting a hard winter this year. Not good for the cars to be out in the cold elements. The single carport isn't going to be big enough for two." She shook her head and then amazed everyone. "Sounds like we need to build a garage," she suggested with a sly look. Her eyes focused on her husband and then looked to her son.

"Mom, are you serious? Does this mean I can keep her? That is if I decide to."

"Yes. But why wouldn't you? The car is a beauty. Also, find out if that good-looking boy is part of the deal," Karen teased.

"I'm not interested," Kaitlyn said, stuffing her mouth with a bite of pancakes to avoid any further discussion in that area.

"Now wait a minute," Seth chimed in. "That's hardly fair. You get a hot car, and Dad and I get stuck working."

"Take it up with mom," Kaitlyn replied with a sly grin. "But you know I will be helping with the garage too. Let's take her for a test drive after the kitchen is clean. Jena and I have clean-up duty this morning."

"Is that a bribe?" Seth asked, questioning her motives.

"Maybe. Besides, I'd like your opinion," Kaitlyn said, attempting to smooth things over.

Jena interrupted, looking at her husband with soft eyes, "I thought we were going to look at a new dishwasher today."

"Oh yeah. I forgot," Seth said, raising his brows. "Ok, after we go shopping, I'll call you, and we will take her for a spin."

"Perfect. But I get to drive her first," Kaitlyn smiled, claiming her place.

"Fine with me. She'll be all warm and ready when it's my turn."

"Ha, ha," Kaitlyn replied with a grin, then turned her attention to Carson and helped him make a mouth on his pancake with chocolate chips.

"He's got black teeth. He needs to go to the dentist," Carson giggled as he ate the chips from the pancake. Then the room broke out into an uproar, and the conversation returned to the group.

After the meal, Jena and Kaitlyn cleared the table and retired into the kitchen. The two enjoyed their girl time while working together.

"OMG!" Jena exclaimed, bumping hips with Kaitlyn at the sink. Her smile wide. "That Jason is such a hunk."

Kaitlyn threw her a frown, "Really? I hadn't noticed."

"Well, then you must be dead. Because he even caused my heart to flutter, and I'm a happily married woman."

"Not dead, just taking a break from men," Kaitlyn replied, handing her a washed dish to rinse.

"You know, it's ok to feel again."

"Maybe someday, but not now. Please, can we change the subject?" Kaitlyn pleaded, her heart not ready to fall and fail again.

3) THE CONNECTION

"Hey Sis," Seth said as he came into the kitchen, his son trailing behind. "Can you watch Carson while we run to town?"

"Of course. How can I resist this cute face?" Kaitlyn said, happy for the interruption from her deep thoughts. She bent down and pinched her nephew's chubby cheeks. "After I'm through, what do you think about taking a stroll around the yard and visiting the animals?"

He jumped in place. "Yes. Can we feed the chickens?" the excited little boy asked.

"Yes. But you'd better find your belt because you wouldn't want the rooster crowing at your underwear," Kaitlyn said.

Carson gave his dad an alarming look. "We need to find my belt," he said, taking his hand, leading him out of the kitchen on a mission.

Jena shook her head and looked at Kaitlyn. "How do you do it? We tried everything, and nothing has worked."

"It's because you're his parents, and I'm his fun aunt."

"Well, you're good with him. Someday you're going to make a great mom. You and that hunk would make beautiful babies," Jena teased.

"Seriously, Jena," Kaitlyn exclaimed playfully, hitting her with the dishtowel.

Three hours later, Kaitlyn walked into her brother's house with a tired little boy, half-asleep in her arms. "He is ready for a nap after our morning adventure," she whispered, then handed him to Seth.

After Seth put his son to bed, he and Kaitlyn headed for the garage.

"I can't believe it's here," Kaitlyn said excitedly, leaning up against the shiny hood. She'd called Jason earlier and thanked him and confirmed they were still on for that afternoon. She also told him to look for the girl driving the beautiful blue T-Bird.

"Mom said the keys were under the mat," Seth said, climbing into the passenger seat.

"Awesome," she replied, retrieving the keys. Before starting the piece of art on wheels, she gazed at the unique style of the interior trim of her, hopefully, new baby. She ran her hand over the smooth vinyl. It was a blend of turquoise-colored bolsters wrapped around the seat cushion's outer edge and separated by a white stripe in the middle. "Look at the distinctive sewing pattern on the seats. It's only found in a few models. Just think Seth, this beauty could be mine," Kaitlyn said with enthusiasm, dancing in the seat. After taking a deep breath to reign in her giddy emotions, she adjusted the mirrors and seat, and familiarized herself with the array of operational controls, switches, dials, and gauges. "Ok, ready?" she said, inserted the key and turned it to start. But the anticipated rumble of the engine was replaced by the disappointing sound of a hollow click.

Kaitlyn stared at her brother with a perplexed look. "Must be a little cold." After pumping the gas pedal a few times, she tried again, only to get the same result.

"You think it's out of gas?" she said in exasperation, grabbing the steering wheel with both hands.

Seth shook his head. "No, I don't know Jason, but my gut tells me he wouldn't bring it over empty. Here, trade places with me and let me give it a go," Seth offered as he stepped out of the car.

"Ok. If you think you have the magic touch, go for it."

Seth took his place in the driver's seat, turned the key, and the car started right up. "I guess I do," he boasted.

"Show off. Ok, I can take it from here." She tugged on his shirt to get out the car.
"Just listen to the purr of that engine," she swooned as she started backing up. The car hesitated and sputtered a few times before dying out.

"Are you kidding me?" expressed a frustrated Kaitlyn.

"Maybe she doesn't like you," Seth teased, looking at his distressed sister.

Kaitlyn threw him a snarly look. "She's just a little cold, that's all." Then she rubbed her hands together to prepare for another attempt to start the temperamental vehicle.

"Come on, baby," she pleaded while turning the key, and again nothing. "Argh," Kaitlyn fumed, hitting the steering wheel.

"Now, now. That's no way to treat her, especially if she isn't fond of you."

"Really!" she said, glaring at her brother, her irritation level rising.

"Let me try it again," he offered, dismissing her temper.

"Fine!" she snapped, stepping away from the car.

"Watch this." With his hands linked together in front, Seth cracked his knuckles.

Kaitlyn rolled her eyes at her brother. "Just start it already."

Again, the car started up with ease. "Why don't I drive it down the road, get her warmed up, and then I'll turn it over to you?"

"Might as well," Kaitlyn said, plopping down in the passenger seat, her arms crossed at her chest. She soon relaxed as they drove down the highway. She embraced the refreshing wind through the open window, closed her eyes, and focused on the hum of the engine.

As promised, Seth pulled off the road and they switched places. But as soon as she pushed the gas pedal, the car died. "This is ridiculous," she shrieked.

"Maybe you have negative energy, which is killing the engine."

"Yeah, that's it," she replied sarcastically.

"I'm sorry, Sis. I know that sounds lame, but I don't have any other explanation for it."

"Why don't you just take me home," Kaitlyn said, folding her arms at her chest.

"Sure. If that's what you want," Seth said as he turned the vehicle around and headed back to the house.

"Guess I'll have to call Jason and tell him we can't meet today."

"What do you mean the car won't let you drive it?" Jason asked after he listened to Kaitlyn's explanation.

"I know it sounds crazy, but I have my brother as a witness. I've tried multiple times, it won't start for me, and when it's running, the car dies on me."

"Hmm, that is very strange," Jason commented. "I'll come over there and check it out, but my mechanical skills are limited. We can also drive to my uncle's shop. There must be a logical reason this is happening. See you in a bit."

Kaitlyn met Jason at her garage promptly at 4:00. She greeted him with a smile and handed him the keys. "The stubborn girl is all yours."

"Why don't you give her a go," he said, refusing the keys. "I want to see for myself what is happening. Not sure if it will make a difference, but it couldn't hurt."

"Ok," Kaitlyn said as she got in the car and attempted to start it. And just like before, nothing happened. "See, I told you, it won't start for me."

Jason scratched his head as he pondered the situation. "I don't understand. You press on the gas, and I will turn the key."

Kaitlyn followed Jason's instructions, and the car started right up. But when she stepped on the gas, the car died out again.

"I don't get it," Jason said as he shook his head. "But it doesn't surprise me too much," he added, turning toward Kaitlyn. "When dad first got the car, he spent weeks in the barn with it. Wouldn't let us near it at first, and I could always hear him talking to it."

"What was he saying to it?" Kaitlyn asked, the subject piquing her interest.

"I don't know. My dad's voice was always low. It was as though he didn't want anyone to hear," Jason admitted. "This may seem crazy, but maybe I should try and talk to her."

"Sure, good luck with that," Kaitlyn replied with an odd look.

"Unless you have any other ideas you'd like to share."

"No, she's all yours," Kaitlyn replied with an entertained look.

Jason lowered his head to the hood. "Tatiana, Jason here, Greg's son. I've never spoken to a car before, and to tell you the truth, I feel quite foolish, but if it worked for my dad, maybe it will for me. Not sure what to say or even how much you understand, but here it goes. I'd appreciate it if you'd be cooperative for Kaitlyn. I think you two would be a good match, and she'd take good care of you, so please give her a try. I'd hate to have to put you back in the barn and cover you up."

Kaitlyn grinned. She did find it humorous he was speaking directly to the car and giving her a sweet yet tactful ultimatum. "What next? Are you going to sing to her?"

"Go ahead and try it again," he said, disregarding her sarcastic comment.

"If I have to," Kaitlyn replied with a sigh. The first time she heard a click, but after the second attempt, the car turned over, and the engine rumbled. "I can't believe it. What just really happened? Is this some magic trick? Did you push a button?" she asked, baffled, looking around for anything suspicious. There was no way she wanted to think the car could understand what Jason was saying.

"I swear I did nothing," Jason said, raising his hands. "I'm as amazed as you are. Maybe there is something special about this car. I wonder...," he said as he rubbed his hand over the dash.

"Wonder what?"

"Maybe she knows what happened to my dad? Do you know, girl?" At that question, the song *"Country Roads"* blasted out of the radio.

"What's happening?" Kaitlyn shrieked as she changed the station and turned down the volume. "That was very weird." Then she put the car in gear and drove onto the road.

"She does drive nicely," Kaitlyn said, enjoying the car. "So, are we still on for coffee?"

"I'm game if you are. We can take a long way. It will give you more time to cruise."

"I like that," Kaitlyn replied as she glanced over at Jason. For the first time, the young man caught her eye. Jena was right. He was handsome. No, he was downright hot, she thought, immediately pulling her eyes away. "OMG," she thought. "This isn't good, not good at all. Keep your eyes on the road and drive," she instructed herself, turning away from her sexy shotgun rider.

Kaitlyn pulled into a parking lot and found a spot in front. After she turned off the engine, a strange man approached her window, lowered his sunglasses, and commented, "Sweet ride." He then poked his head in to get a closer look.

"Thanks," Kaitlyn replied as she leaned her body back against the seat.

"Is it yours?" the man asked, his elbows leaning on the window.

"Working on it," she answered politely.

"Well, if you ever want to get rid of it, I'll take it off your hands. Here's my number," the stranger said, stepping away from the car and reaching into his pocket. Then after tossing his head to the side to swoop his hair out of his eyes, he handed Kaitlyn a business card. "Hey, if you'd like to get coffee or hang out, you can call me anytime. I'm Simon, and you are?" the guy asked, probing for information.

"She's with me," Jason said. He didn't know why but this guy hitting on her bothered him, and he could tell she was uncomfortable with his forwardness.

"Hey, sorry, man. I don't want any trouble. You two have a good day," he said with a two-finger salute and walked away.

"Thanks," Kaitlyn said. "That guy was giving me the creeps," she confessed, shaking off the eerie feeling. "Shall we go in?"

She grabbed her purse, but before she could get out of the car the horn started blaring, which startled her, causing Simon's card to go flying.

"What are you doing?" Jason yelled over the noise.

"Nothing," she replied.

"Then why is it sounding off like that?" he yelled while covering his ears.

"I don't know. Why don't you ask Tatiana? You can speak car," Kaitlyn commented with a fake smile as she placed her hands over her ears.

"Very funny," Jason replied with a tilt of his head. "I'll look under the hood. Maybe I can disconnect it."

"Good luck," she said and then slumped down in her seat, hoping to hide from the curious group of people gathering around the vehicle.

Jason found what he thought was the wire going to the horn and yanked on it until it was free. However, the noise continued. Frustrated, and with a headache in the making, Jason spoke softly but sternly to the car. "Tatiana, this behavior is inexcusable. If you continue, I will put you back in the barn." Instantly the sound stopped. "Thank you," Jason said as he closed the hood.

After Kaitlyn made sure the people had found something else to entertain themselves with, she got out of the car. "That was wild. "What did you do?"

"Simple. I threatened to put her in the barn again," Jason answered as he opened the door to the café.

"Seriously?" Kaitlyn asked, walking into the establishment. The smell of coffee and pastries filling the air tempted her palate and sweet tooth. However, she decided to pass on the sugary treats. The pancakes drowned in syrup for breakfast had been enough sugar to hold her cravings for a while, well, at least a day or two.

Jason escorted her to the order line, making sure he kept a protective watch on her. "Why don't I order while you find a table. What can I get you?"

"Tall vanilla latte," she replied, then set out to find a seat. Luckily, Sunday afternoon left many empty tables. Kaitlyn opted for one in the back, away from the gawking stares. She recognized a few faces from the crowd who had gathered around her car during the horn incident.

Ten minutes later, Jason returned with their order and took a seat across from Kaitlyn. "My ears are still ringing from the noise," he admitted, shaking his head.

"Are you sure it stopped on its own?"

"Positive. I had already pulled the wire. Technically, that should have instantly cut the horn," Jason said with a confused look. "You know, I'm beginning to think there is something special about that car. I also believe my dad knew that, as well."

"It all seems so crazy," Kaitlyn said as she swirled her coffee with the straw.

Jason looked away as he spoke, "I was never around her by myself. Dad always made sure he was there. He kept the barn locked, which seemed odd to mom and me, but we never pushed the subject. We figured his fixation, almost obsession, would pass after a while," Jason said, blowing on the hot liquid before taking a sip. "So, why classic cars?" he asked.

"That's easy. They're not polluted with computers and technical accessories. It makes maintenance easier, and you know exactly how the car operates." she said, taking a sip through the straw.

"I never thought about them like that," Jason replied, seeing her passion for cars in her eyes.

Kaitlyn continued, "The insides have clean lines, and the panels aren't cluttered with knobs and buttons. They usually contain only the necessary accessories. You can also assume the cars have had more than one owner.

Thus, many secrets and stories remain locked in the interior."

"Hmm, I wonder if that is why my dad was so into them," Jason surmised.

"Are classic cars your thing, like your dad?" Kaitlyn asked with interest.

"Not really," he admitted. "I just pretended so I could hang out with him. I can fake the talk enough to make conversation, and have enough mechanical experience to be dangerous, but the passion is not there." Then Jason took another sip of his coffee and stared out the window.

Kaitlyn could tell talking about his dad was painful, and she felt sad for him. "I'm sorry, we can change the subject," she offered. A desire rose inside her to reach out and touch him, but she pulled back from the impulse.

"Thank you. It's all good, at least as good as it can be. Mom says it's healthy to talk about him. I tend to suppress and bury my feelings. I want to think my dad is still alive, and now I wonder if that car really does know something," he responded sincerely.

Kaitlyn didn't know what to think about his comment. She couldn't fathom the possibility, but she could play along to humor him. "What do you think it could know?"

"I don't know. Now that you have Tatiana, maybe you can help me find out what it knows about my dad's disappearance."

"Help you how?" she asked in a high-pitched voice. She then laughed at the absurdity of the conversation. "Even if

I thought she could somehow communicate, which I don't, haven't you noticed? We're not exactly friends."

"Yeah, that's right," Jason said as he raked his fingers through his curls. "I'll have another talk with her at your house before I leave."

Oh yeah, that will work, Kaitlyn thought. She was thankful they were seated away from prying ears. Their conversation was speeding down the looney-tune highway and gaining momentum. She was having a difficult time comprehending a car could have feelings. "I don't know,"' Kaitlyn said with a sigh. "You don't think the car has special powers, do you?" she asked and sent him a curious look.

"I don't know what to think," he said, resting his forehead in his palms. "You have to admit Tatiana started after I spoke to her, the horn also stopped, and the song started on the car stereo."

Kaitlyn twisted her mouth. "Maybe it was just a coincidence," she said, not ready to concede.

"I don't think so. Something tells me there's more to that car than just metal and tires. I'm going to figure out what makes her tick. You did say cars have many secrets."

Kaitlyn smiled, picked up her cup, and stared at him over the rim. "I'll give it some thought. But I'm not going to make any promises."

"I'll take it. Are you about ready? I promised my mom I'd be home for dinner."

"I'm ready."

"Can we stop at the store on the way? I need to pick up some yellow roses. I have another apology to make. I said some terrible things to her, and the pain in her eyes haunted me all night. I just don't know what came over me," Jason admitted.

"Don't be too hard on yourself. I'm sure your mom understands." This time Kaitlyn didn't hesitate and reached out and put her hand on his arm, but then immediately pulled it away.

"Yes, but she doesn't deserve it. She's already suffering. That is why it's so important that I find out what happened." Jason rubbed his arm still tingling from her touch. He shook off the awkward feeling and let it go. He had no intention of getting involved.

"Ok, I'm in," Kaitlyn replied in the heat of moment. She couldn't bear to see the sadness in his eyes. "C'mon let's go. You don't want to keep your mom waiting."

The next morning, Kaitlyn stood under the carport next to Tatiana and tried hard to believe it was different from all other cars. That was as far as her mind was willing to go. The thought of it being alive or that it could somehow relate, comprehend, and respond was beyond her wildest imagination. Cars just couldn't do that. At least not in her world.

Yesterday, in a moment of unforeseen compassion and caught up in the desperate look in Jason's eyes, she'd felt committed, an impulsive moment of madness for sure. Realizing she couldn't back down, she deliberated on the complicated issue all during the night. Finally deciding, under another moment of madness, to reach out to the car and see what would happen.

Kaitlyn stared at the car and wondered if she'd made the right decision or if Jason's crazy ideas were overtaking her thinking. The worst that could happen was the car would do nothing, and she'd be back where she started. Maybe by some miracle, beyond the laws of nature, the car would prove her wrong. That was both an exciting and frightening thought.

Before Kaitlyn climbed into the car, she touched the hood and the memory of the temperature change popped into her mind, and wondered if there was something special about this car. "Hi, Tatiana. I'm probably your least favorite person right now. I've taken you from your home and put you in this strange place. You don't have to worry. If they find your owner, I will give you back." Kaitlyn paused for a moment, giving Tatiana a chance to respond, and was half-way relieved when the car remained still and silent. Even though she felt silly, Kaitlyn continued her talk. "We will probably never be best friends, but I hope we can become traveling companions. I will try to help you find your owner. However, I don't know what that involves currently. With that, please start for me and let me drive you," Kaitlyn pleaded as she opened the car door.

After taking a deep breath and saying a silent prayer, Kaitlyn inserted the key and turned it to start. She smiled, but was also a little freaked out, when the car started with no trouble. Had Tatiana understood what she'd said, or was it just a coincidence? At any rate, Kaitlyn patted the dashboard and commented, "Thank you. It's such a nice day. Let's put the top down and then head to Bill's Automotive and Towing in town."

Kaitlyn silently celebrated as she pulled out onto the highway. She had made progress and strangely felt a slight connection with the car. Everything was going smoothly until she reached a four-way stop, and the car took control and forced Kaitlyn to go right instead of left. "Tatiana, what are you doing? We are not going the right way," she said, her hand wrestling with the moving steering wheel and trying to regain control of the car. "I have a meeting with Bill in a few minutes. We don't have time for any detours. Where are you taking me?" Kaitlyn asked as the car took off on its own.

Finally, a red light forced her to stop. Thank goodness Tatiana follows the road rules, she thought. Just when Kaitlyn had assumed she'd won the battle, the crazy car decided to challenge some kids in a cherry-red, souped-up Chevy Camaro. The racing of the engines matched the pounding in her chest as she grabbed tight to the steering wheel, bracing herself for a scary ride.

4) FIRST DAY AT THE SHOP

"No, Tatiana. Bad car!" Kaitlyn scolded, turning her head to hide her face from the excited kids. When the light changed, she pushed down hard on the brakes and pulled the emergency brake for extra precaution. She hoped that it would hold the car back. Fortunately, Kaitlyn was able to restrain the vehicle and casually waved as the screeching hot rod flew past her.

When the car was out of sight, Kaitlyn wrestled with the steering wheel and maneuvered Tatiana safely through the green light and parked on the shoulder. She breathed a heavy sigh and, when her heartbeat was back to normal, set some ground rules with Tatiana. "Listen here, Missy. There will be no road games, and I'll decide where we go. I have agreed to help you. So, the least you can do is be cooperative. I've got only a few minutes to make it to Bill's. Please don't fight me on this," Kaitlyn pleaded. She was relieved to be able to turn the car around. "Thank you, Tati."

Kaitlyn's eyes filled with surprise when she pulled into Bill's and spotted Jason checking out her Volkswagen Bug, Sunny. He greeted her with a smile as she approached him. "Hi, what are you doing here?"

"Hey," Jason replied. He stood, stunned, with his mouth gaping as he watched her get out of the car. The floral sundress, exposing the most stunning pair of flawless legs, left him speechless. He would need to be careful, or he'd let that sassy redhead walk right into his personal life. That was something he couldn't allow. So, after finding his voice, Jason continued, "In between plumbing assignments, I help my uncle. He has more work than he can handle, but not enough to hire a full-time employee."

"That's extremely sweet. I thought you didn't know much about cars?" Kaitlyn inquired.

"I can do minor things."

"So, I guess you're not going to be operating on Sunny?" Kaitlyn teased as she patted the car's hood.

Jason snickered. "Not if you want to drive her again." He then closed the hood and stared at Kaitlyn. "Hey, don't you think jeans would be more suited for this type of environment?"

Kaitlyn questioned him with a smirk as she spun around. "What, you don't like my dress?"

"I didn't say that. The dress is great, legs are great." Then Jason stopped when he realized he'd spoken without a filter. "What I mean is you wouldn't want to ruin such a pretty dress."

Kaitlyn covered her mouth to hide a smile. But she was sure the redness in her cheeks showed her embarrassment.

"I'd better go. I'm meeting Bill in about five minutes," she replied. Kaitlyn wanted to put some distance between them, and quick.

"Oh yeah, about that. Bill said to tell you he's running behind and will be available in about fifteen minutes."

Kaitlyn let out a long sigh. "I'll just wait in the car," she said, turning to leave.

Jason could tell his slip of the tongue had left them both feeling uncomfortable, so he quickly changed the subject. "So, it looks like my talk with Tatiana worked," he sneered with overconfidence.

Kaitlyn stopped and replied smugly, "Or maybe it was mine."

"I thought you didn't believe the car could communicate."

"Well..., I might've changed my mind. I do have that prerogative. You know us girls have to stick together," she flicked a short curl and chuckled.

"I'm happy you two are getting along."

"Yeah, I guess you could say that" Kaitlyn replied. She wasn't about to tell him about her recent adventure. It had been a bump in the road. Hopefully now she and Tatiana had reached an understanding.

"Well, I'd better get back to work," Jason commented.

"Yeah, I should go wait for Bill. See ya later."

"I'll call you, and maybe we can get together."

"Uh, sure," Kaitlyn replied apprehensively, wondering if he was asking her out.

"To talk about a plan to find my dad."

"Oh yes. Right," Kaitlyn said, turning her head to hide the disappointment on her face. She wasn't sure if she was relieved or upset that it wasn't a date.

Forty-five minutes later, Kaitlyn came out of Bill's office, twirling a key ring on her fingers and a work schedule in her hands. She had agreed to Mondays, Wednesdays, and Fridays from eight till three and every other Saturday. Her first day of work would be this Wednesday. She had managed to negotiate $15.00 an hour. He bravely lent her his credit card, with a set limit, to fix up the office. Kaitlyn was excited at the opportunity to redo the small space. However, she wasn't thrilled about cleaning the area. At least Bill had removed everything from the counter and placed all the items in a box. She'd need to get busy and have the office somewhat acceptable in two days.
Painting the walls could wait until later. Maybe she could bribe Jason into helping.

Two awfully long days later, an exhausted Kaitlyn poured her wilted body into her chair and celebrated the updated office. She had spent many hours scrubbing and cleaning. She had replaced the sofa and coffee stand, then added a gray throw rug in front of the door. The counter now held a filing basket, business cards in a holder, and a stack of part books. Jason and Bill had washed the walls, which were now bare. They would stay like that until they were painted. She and Bill were in a debate over what posters would go back up. Yes, she could work here, Kaitlyn thought. She then pulled her tired self from the chair, took one last look, turned off the light, and locked the door.

Kaitlyn flinched when the radio in the car automatically came on. Ever since she'd bought the car, random songs would pop on without warning. They were always from various stations and music types. Today it was country again. She listened carefully to the words, *"The sharp knife of a short life."* "What does that mean Tati? I don't understand," Kaitlyn admitted with a head shake. "Are you trying to tell me something?" she asked. Then she remembered yesterday's song selection: *"Every girl's crazy about a sharp-dressed man,"* but she still couldn't come up with a connection. Hopefully, the car would reveal more soon, she thought.

That evening, Kaitlyn joined her family for dinner. It was their tradition that each member took turns sharing about their day. If someone was having a bad day, the family often tried to raise their spirits and turn the day around for them. Tonight, Kaitlyn tried to hide the confusion in her eyes and give her attention to the conversations. But in her mind, she was still trying to decipher the meaning of the song lyrics. Occasionally she'd draw someone's eye contact and briefly pay more attention to a topic, just to act engaged. She didn't want to let on that her thoughts were tangled up with the mysterious car.

Jason called her around 9:00 PM, and when the call ended, she couldn't believe they'd talked for nearly an hour. Mostly they gabbed about the car and his dad. That was fine with her, as she wasn't ready to drive down Personal Alley yet. She was confident he was also comfortable in that same lane.

The next morning, Kaitlyn woke promptly at 6:10 AM. She hit the snooze alarm only once. If the alarm clock didn't get her up, Gina was her back up. She wouldn't allow her to fall back to sleep. After Kaitlyn showered, she put on her dress jeans, a light blue sweater, and black flats. This work attire was much more fun than the stuffy suits and work dresses that were mandated for her accounting position. Her two-week staycation from that job would be done on Sunday. Then, with the hours at Bill's, she'd be back to work full time. That was going to take time to get used to. After Kaitlyn dropped Gina off at her mom's, she was on her way by 7:15 AM.

The sun was shining, a perfect top-down day. She loved to feel her hair whipping across her face and the warmth of the sun kissing her shoulders. Her senses were in-tune with the elements. There were no side windows to block her view. She could hear the birds singing and smell the roadside wildflowers. She soon learned that there were a few disadvantages to driving so freely, such as the need to keep her mouth closed to avoid eating bugs and hold her breath while passing a millpond. Since Tatiana had been cooperative ever since the incident yesterday, Kaitlyn decided to give her control of the car for a few minutes. She felt it might provide a bonding moment between them.

Everything was fine until Kaitlyn spotted a stretch of irrigation sprays crossing the highway and realized Tati was headed straight for the fountains. "Stop the car this instant," Kaitlyn demanded with an open-mouthed stare. "If we go through there, we are going to get soaked."

It hit her that Tatiana had no intention of stopping. In her haste, she grabbed a paper bag lying in the seat and placed it on her head. She hoped, by some miracle, it would protect her from the large drops of water.

Kaitlyn clenched her jaw, and fury burned in her eyes as she called the car many choice names over the loud sounds of the sprinklers. The bag was worthless. Like she had anticipated, she was now drenched from head to toe. When they reached the dry pavement, Tati pulled over to the side of the road. Kaitlyn could swear she heard laughter coming from the car.

"Oooh, Tati!" Kaitlyn screamed as she tried to pat herself with the remains of the saturated sack. "Now, you stop! That wasn't funny, and it was not a smart move. Not only did you try to drown me, but you also managed to soak your carpets. I'm supposed to report to work in thirty minutes, and I'm literally a wet mess." Kaitlyn crushed the remains of the paper bag in her fist and tossed it on the floor. After she gained control of her temper, Kaitlyn spoke softly but assertively to the vehicle. "Give me back control of MY car. Or tonight, I'll cover you up and lock you in the garage with your top on."

Kaitlyn crouched in her seat when she pulled into the shop parking spot and saw Jason standing by the office door. She certainly didn't want him to see her in this condition, but it was unavoidable, and there was nowhere for her to hide. Maybe he wouldn't notice, she thought, fooling herself.

She smoothed down her hair with her hand, put on her best smile, and stepped out of the car.
Jason walked over to Kaitlyn with his mouth wide open. "What happened?" he asked. "Why are you and the interior of the car soaked?"

"We went through an irrigation spray."

"Hmm, you probably should've put the top on. There is a pool of water on the back floor."

"Really? Tell that to The Diva."

"I wish you two would get along."

"I did nothing wrong. Tatiana is a spoiled brat with a stubborn streak," Kaitlyn shrieked, her hands forcefully twisting her blouse. She watched in anger as small pools of water formed at her feet.

Jason shook his head, "Girl," he sighed, "what's that in your hair?"

"Oh no. Is it a spider or bee? I don't like either of them," Kaitlyn screeched as her feet jumped in place.

"I don't think so. It looks like a French fry," Jason said as he reached over and pulled out the soggy potato and showed it to her. "Was it also raining fries?" he asked with a cockeyed grin.

"Ha, ha. I'm not in the mood," Kaitlyn snapped. She shook her head to remove any other leftover lunch items that may be stuck in her hair.

"Ok," Jason said, trying hard not to laugh as the spray from her hair hit his face. "Then I won't ask how the red streak that looks a lot like ketchup got in your hair either."

"Probably a good idea," she said, sending him a glare. "The problem is, I can't even punish her," Kaitlyn expressed with frustration.

"I'll talk to her again," Jason volunteered. "Now, you'd better get cleaned up. Bill is due back shortly, and the shop opens in twenty minutes."

Kaitlyn tilted her head and gave him a funny look. "I have nothing to change into, and there's not enough time for me to run home. I'm just going to have to suffer through it."

"I have a clean work shirt in the car and a baseball cap. It's not much, but you are welcome to them."

Kaitlyn smiled. She didn't want to like this guy, but he kept doing such nice things, and it was hard to resist his boyish charm. "Thanks, I'd appreciate that. It's my best offer yet."

He looked around and shrugged, "Seems like it's your only one. I'll run and get them and watch the shop while you are freshening up," he offered with a slight grin.

A few minutes later, Kaitlyn moaned as she took in her replacement attire. The over-sized black light-weight flannel fit her like a dress. The extra-long sleeves rolled up her arms only added to the beauty. Her jeans were still a little damp, but she could live with that. To top it off, her hair, now a sticky mess, was tucked inside a black ballcap. The cap had a bright yellow logo which, she guessed, was his favorite baseball team. "Well, here goes my first day, and probably my last," she said with a sigh as she stepped out of the restroom.

"Not bad," Jason commented as he tried to cover up his intake of breath. He wasn't prepared to see Kaitlyn in his clothes. Something stirred inside him, and it was an emotion he didn't want to feel, so he pushed it aside.

"Something right out of the farmer's almanac," she said with a false smile.

"I think you're dressed perfectly for the job," he said. He thought it was better than the sundress she had on the other day. No exposed legs to drive him or anyone else crazy. He wondered to himself, why should that matter? "You'll be fine," Jason said. He playfully pulled the ball cap over her eyes. "I'd better get to work and get the water out of Tatiana. Good luck on your first day, slugger. I'll call you later."

"Sure, later," she said. Kaitlyn then adjusted the ballcap, took her place behind the counter, and prepared for their first customer.

Bill walked into the shop close to 10:00 AM, and didn't mention her appearance. In fact, he pointed to the cap and said, "Great team." She went over with him the call messages and a couple of invoices. He shook his head and told her he couldn't get over how great the shop looked and teased her about cleaning his home. Then, he handed her a package and told her it was for his friend, John. "Do you have any questions I can answer before I head to the garage?"

Kaitlyn shook her head. "Not now. It's been a slow morning. I had time to go over your books and get familiar with your purchasing software. I feel it could use an upgrade. Also, I checked your website. I have some ideas that will get more people to visit your site. If you like, I could update it for you."

"Hmm. How much would that cost?" Bill asked cautiously.

"I'm sure we can negotiate a fair rate," she said with her infectious grin.

"Why not," Bill replied, handing her a notepad. "You put together something, and I'll look at it this weekend. I'd better get to work. The meeting this morning has already cost me a few dollars. Oh, by the way, the parts for Sunny should be here today. The UPS guy usually arrives after 2:00 PM. If you need anything, call the garage number."

Over the next couple of hours, Kaitlyn struggled to keep up with the steady flow of customers. She hadn't had enough time to learn all the procedures and processes, and she didn't want to bother Bill. His shop didn't sell many auto parts. He did, however, have connections to various shops, and he knew where to obtain classic car parts that were outdated. These connections and his knowledge brought people in. She apologized for being slow, and for the most part, everyone had been considerate and understanding. However, there had been one man who'd been a little agitated with her when she had made a tiny mistake. He'd needed a part for his pick-up, and she'd accidentally ordered a piece for a hobby car instead. She thought it was funny, but he did not. Luckily, Kaitlyn was able to promptly fix the problem.

She welcomed the busyness and chaos, as it kept her mind from wandering to Jason. Ever since she'd put on his shirt and hat, Katilyn felt a closeness toward him. This feeling both scared and excited her. It was a dangerous place for her to go. She closed and locked that feeling behind an imaginary door in her mind. The problem was, she couldn't wash away his scent, lingering on his shirt.
At noon, Kaitlyn hung the Out-to-Lunch sign in the window and drove into town to grab a salad. Thankfully, there hadn't been any more incidents with Tatiana. In fact,

the car almost acted normal. But at the same time, that felt strange. Kaitlyn knew that this quiet time was only temporary and wondered what the car would be up to next. It was like the calm before the storm.

Then, as if Tatiana had read her mind, a song blasted through the radio. Kaitlyn shivered as she listened to the words, *"Come on, Pretty Baby, Kiss Me Deadly."* "Oh, Tati," she expressed in horror. She immediately changed the station with her shaking hand.

There was a man waiting for her at the door when she returned to work. She greeted him with a smile while unlocking the door. "How can I help you?" she asked the tall and lean gentleman as she stepped behind the counter.

"Morning, Miss," he kindly said as he tipped his cowboy hat. This exposed his weathered face and a patch of gray hair. "Bill ordered a part for me, John Walls."

"This one must be for you," she said, handing him the large box.

"That sure is a pretty car out there."

"Thanks," Kaitlyn replied as she rang up his order.

"I used to know the owner," he said, signing his receipt.

"I'm sorry. It's so sad they've never found him."

"Him?" John said with a questioning look. "I remember it belonging to a lovely young lady. She used to come into the diner I owned ages ago," he smirked. "I think her name was Tanya or Tina. I'm certain it started with a T. My memory isn't quite a sharp as it used to be."

Kaitlyn could feel a prickle of ice shoot up her spine. She thought, *could it be?* After she swallowed and wet her dry mouth with a drink of water, she asked, "Was it by chance...Tatiana?"

5) SIMON

John snapped his fingers. "Yes, that's it. How did you know?" he asked.

"Lucky guess," she shrugged. "What happened to her? That is if you don't mind my asking."

"Not at all," John said. He walked over to the coffee bar. "It's no secret. All I remember is the car was a birthday gift from her parents. They had arranged a surprise party for her at the Falls.
Tatiana headed up there right after work, expecting to meet up with some friends." John paused while he fixed his coffee. "She never arrived."

"Why?" Kaitlyn asked, afraid she already knew the answer.

John shook his head. "No one knows what happened. The authorities found the car two miles away on a deserted pull-out with no sign of Tatiana. There was never any evidence to show what happened. So, it just became another cold case," John said with a furrowed look. "The library's archives will have the entire story in the Daily Times."

"Oh my!" Kaitlyn exclaimed, then covered her mouth.

"What's wrong, Miss? You look like you've seen a ghost."

"More like uncovered one," Kaitlyn said through gritted teeth.

"I don't understand," John replied.

"One moment." Kaitlyn paused their conversation when the UPS guy came into the shop. She had an uncomfortable feeling about the man with sunglasses and a hoodie covering most of his face. It was probably nothing, she thought. All the talk about Tatiana had her worked up. She signed the form, had the guy set the large box in the corner, and turned her attention back to John.

"Well, to make a long story short, I bought the car from the previous owner, Greg. A similar thing happened to him. The car was found, and Greg was missing. Do you think it was a coincidence?" she asked.

"Of course. Probably not even related," John said with assurance as he headed for the door.

"You're right; it's just my imagination getting ramped up," she said. But deep down, that wasn't how she felt. After John left, Kaitlyn glanced out the window and gasped as she watched him pass by Tatiana. The crazy car's emergency lights started flashing, and the windshield wipers turned on at warp speed. John was oblivious to the car's actions. For Kaitlyn, Tatiana's behavior had her blood pumping and her mind wondering. Was it possible evil lurked within the doors of the vehicle? Was it responsible for the disappearance of Tatiana and Greg and planning her demise as well? She rubbed the goosebumps dancing on her arms and spoke aloud, "Don't be silly. That only happens in horror movies, not real life." Her self-talk, however, did nothing for her confidence. She planned to keep alert and have a firm hold on the steering wheel from now on.

By 5:30 PM, Kaitlyn was ready to be done with her day. She'd called Jason earlier and asked him to meet her at the library in hopes they could find the newspaper article about the young girl's disappearance. She took a deep breath to calm her nerves before climbing into the car. Kaitlyn didn't want Tatiana to sense her fear. "Hey, girl. Let's go to the library," she said in an upbeat tone to hide her nervousness.

"So, tell me again. What are we doing here at the library?" Jason asked. His heart racing as he stood next to Kaitlyn.

As they walked to the microfiche section, Kaitlyn filled Jason in on what John had told her. She was already having difficulty trying to piece together all the clues, and this new information only made her confusion worse. And by the look on Jason's face, it was clear he was also having a hard time digesting all the news.

"The article should be here somewhere. John wasn't sure of the exact year but believed it was in the late '90s," Kaitlyn stated and sat down at a computer table.

"That's a lot of newspapers to review," Jason whined as he sat at the adjoining table.

"True," she replied with a nod, already focusing her attention on the computer screen.

Two hours later, Kaitlyn stood and stretched. "I don't think my eyes or body can take another minute."

"I'm with you," Jason replied as he rolled his neck. "Let's grab some dinner at a food truck and come back tomorrow."

Kaitlyn hesitated and thought of all the reasons why that would not be a good idea.

Jason sensed her uncertainty. "We have to eat, and I'd prefer having company."

"I guess. It's late, I'm hungry, and won't feel like cooking when I get home. I'll meet you there."
Tatiana startled Kaitlyn with another strange set of song lyrics. "*School's out forever,*" blasted out of the speakers. She turned the loud noise down. "What's your story, Tati?" But as usual, the car remained silent.

When Kaitlyn arrived at the food truck, she took off the hat and tried to fix her wild hair. After wasting time playing with the sticky mess, attempting to finger style a suitable style, she concluded it wasn't fixable, put the cap back on, then joined Jason in the short line waiting to order.

They both decided on the burrito supreme and sat at a quaint covered table. Kaitlyn found it was easy to talk with Jason. As they spoke, she realized they had lots in common. They liked many of the same foods, music, movies, and more. He was also funny and made her laugh. If she weren't careful, it would be easy to fall for him. If she kept the talk light and didn't let it get too personal, she'd be safe. Yeah, keep telling yourself that, her conscience interjected. Kaitlyn broke the awkward feeling and told him about the most recent song lyrics.

"What do you think they mean?" Jason asked.

"I think she's trying to tell us what happened."

"Like what? None of it makes sense," Jason stated with confusion.

"Hmm," Kaitlyn mumbled, her fingernails tapping on the table. "Maybe she was murdered by a man dressed in a sharp-looking business suit. Possibly with a knife."

"That's good detective work. Very impressive for a girl," he teased.

"I don't know if a 'girl' is qualified to answer your questions," she replied, emphasizing the word girl with air quotes.

"Seriously, how do you think the 'school's out' fits in?"

"I'm really clueless," Kaitlyn admitted, pursing her lips.

"Ok, let's say your theory is right. Where do we begin?"

"Sorry, Jason, I don't know the answer. We can hope she plays more clues." She looked at her phone. "It's almost 10:00 PM, and I have to work tomorrow. Shall we meet at the library again after work?"

"Sure. I'm game."

"Do you need your clothes back tonight?" Kaitlyn asked as she reached for the ballcap.

"Nah, I'll get them later. It could be your signature look at the shop," Jason teased.

Kaitlyn rolled her eyes. "I think I'll pass. Thanks for the loan. You saved me today."

"Anytime," he replied with a boyish grin.

Jason walked Kaitlyn to her car and opened the door. He was taken back when she kissed him on the cheek.

"Good night," she said, then smiled and climbed behind the wheel of Tati.

Jason stood there, frozen in place with his hand on his cheek, and watched while she drove away.

Kaitlyn couldn't believe she had kissed him. Being bold was never her strong suit. The move was way out of character for her. At least she aimed for the cheek instead of his mouth. She fantasized for a moment. "No, no, no! You're not going there," Kaitlyn scolded herself. Life would be so much simpler if he would only just annoy her.

The drive into work, the following day was uneventful. Kaitlyn was a little disappointed when Jason wasn't there to greet her. She was getting used to seeing him and felt excited to see him later that day. These feeling were not good, she thought.

Bill was at the desk when she walked in. He looked up, "I thought you weren't working on Thursdays."

Kaitlyn put her purse behind the counter and replied, "Only today. Next week I'll be back on my regular schedule. "

"I'm glad you're here. We've only been open for a few minutes, and I've already booked two appointments and answered three phone calls. The desk is all yours," Bill said, stepping out from behind the counter. "I need to get busy before I get further behind. Sorry, Sunny will have to wait a few days."

"No worries, Tatiana is filling her tires. Now go get to work," Kaitlyn giggled and shooed him out the door.

Kaitlyn's eyes were glued to the computer when she heard the bell at the door. Panic hit her like a speeding bullet when she looked up and saw Simon. He was the guy who had practically climbed into her car at the coffee shop. The man had freaked her out then and was doing an even better job of it now that she was alone. Maybe she'd ask Bill to install a silent emergency call button. Sadly enough, that wouldn't help her now. Her dad had taught her to be strong and independent, so she disguised her fear with a fake smile. Simon didn't say much other than introducing himself again. It was the way he looked at her that was sending her over the edge.
Then, as if her nerves weren't already dancing the tango, Tati's horn started going off.

"Excuse me," Kaitlyn said as she shot out the door and raced to her car. Bill arrived before her and was under the hood assessing the problem.

Within a couple of minutes, the noise stopped. Suddenly it occurred to Kaitlyn that Tati might have used her horn to warn Bill and save her. Was it possible she recognized the stranger, or did she sense her fear? "Thank you," she whispered to the car. Her reservations that the car was evil vanished from her mind as she watched the real evil drive away.

"I don't know what caused that. The strange thing is, the horn was already disconnected," Bill confessed with a confused look, rubbing his forehead.

Kaitlyn shrugged her shoulders. She didn't want to share her obscure opinion with Bill as he might not understand. "Thanks for your help," Kaitlyn replied, still working to slow her racing heart. She hadn't realized how much it had affected her until now. "Hey Bill, do you think we could discuss having a panic button installed in your office? There's a guy who may be stalking me, and I'd feel safer if I could alert you."

"Did he come here?" Bill asked, his chest pushed out.

"Yes. He left when Tati's horn sounded."

"You should've called me."

"Well, he didn't threaten me or anything like that. He just gives me the creeps," Kaitlyn said as she crossed her arms and rubbed her goose-bumped arms.

"At any rate, I will call a security company and have one installed. It wouldn't hurt to add a few cameras as well. There's a gun in the drawer below the register just in case I'm not around and that guy threatens you."

"Oh, I hope it doesn't come to that. I'd hate to use it." Kaitlyn trembled at the thought.

"Only an option. You going to be ok?" Bill asked with concern as a father-like softness crossed his face.

"I think so," Kaitlyn replied, her heartbeat back to normal. "Now, don't worry about me. Get back to work."

Kaitlyn went back to the office and tried to hide in her work. Her shaky concentration was easily broken each time the notification bell sounded and someone entered the office. After the morning's incident, her nerves were on overdrive, and they were strung tighter than a taut guitar string. Just when she was wondering how she'd make it through the day, Jason walked in.

"Hey, how's it going?" he asked with a smile.

"Fine. Everything is fine," Kaitlyn lied.

Jason leaned against the counter. "That's not what I was told."

"Did Bill tell you? Well, I don't need a babysitter," she informed him. Even though it was a relief to have him there, she wasn't about to let him see her weak. He'd only want to rescue her. Kaitlyn didn't need that. She could take care of herself.

"He might've mentioned it."

"Well, you've wasted your time. As I said, I'm fine. No, more like awesome," Kaitlyn insisted, grinning ear to ear.

Jason could see Kaitlyn was putting on a show. Her burst of enthusiasm was too dramatic, a plastic smile wasn't convincing, and her eyes showed the buried fear. He didn't want to push. It was easy to see she didn't want to talk. "I'll be outside changing an alternator," he commented.

"Whatever," she replied, then pretended to go back to work.

Jason didn't want to go far. He had been a wreck after he received Bill's phone call. He'd dropped what he was doing and headed straight over. His protective nature fueled his anger. It had taken him only ten minutes to get there, but it felt like an eternity. His racing heart hadn't slowed until he'd found her safe inside the shop. He wasn't used to these new emotions stirring inside him. He decided to push them aside as he applied his energy to his task at hand.

Jason was under a truck when Kaitlyn stepped outside the office. "Hi," she said, bending down to talk to him. "Do you think we could go to the library tomorrow?"

"Of course," Jason replied, scooting out from under the vehicle. "You sure you're ok? And be honest this time."

"Does it show that badly? I admit his presence shook me up. But I think Tatiana recognized him which upset her worse."

"From where?" Jason asked, then stood and wiped his greasy hands on his overalls.

"I don't know," she said with a shrug. "See you tomorrow." Then she hurried to her car to dodge any more questions. All she wanted to do was go home, chill with a glass of wine, and cuddle with her fur-baby. She needed an escape from her traumatic day. The irony was she'd overcome her scary encounter with Mr. Creepy; however, it was Jason tugging on her heartstrings that plagued her thoughts. "My knight in coveralls and work boots," she swooned and patted her heart.

Kaitlyn stopped at her parent's house to pick up Gina, who sat patiently waiting on the porch until she saw her friend, then ran like mad to greet her. Fortunately for Kaitlyn, her parents weren't home. She didn't feel like talking. There was no way to hide her emotions from her mom. She always sensed when something wasn't right. Kaitlyn learned if she avoided eye contact, she could occasionally slip under her mom's radar. But that didn't always work. Since nothing had happened today, there was no need to worry them.

"C'mon girl, let's go home," Kaitlyn called to Gina. "I have a bottle of Chablis calling my name, and I believe there's a steak bone calling yours. We'll go for a long run before dinner."

The next day Kaitlyn woke up early. She wanted time to get in a thirty-minute workout and spend time tossing the ball for Gina. By the time she climbed into the car, her body felt revitalized and her mind centered. "Today is going to be a good day," she said, stating her affirmation. When Kaitlyn pulled into the shop's driveway, she noticed two security vans, her dad's pickup, and Jason's rig crammed in the small area. There was barely enough room for her to park.

Her dad approached her car, and she looked at him with confusion. "Dad, what are you doing here?"

Rob opened the car door, helped Kaitlyn out of the car, and pulled her into his arms. "Bill told me what happened yesterday. You know how your mom is; she wanted me to check on you."

Kaitlyn stepped away and looked at her dad. "Everything is fine, dad. So, you can go home and tell mom there's no reason to worry."

"I think I'll stay for a while," Rob insisted.

"You can't stay here and watch me all day. I'll be fine. I brought my security," Kaitlyn said as she opened the car door to let Gina out, put on her leash and walked past her dad.

Kaitlyn walked into a busy shop and maneuvered her way around a man installing a security camera. She smiled at Bill, who was busy talking with Jason and another security man. She led Gina behind the counter and took in the entire scene.

"Hi," Jason said as he stepped behind the counter.

Kaitlyn waited to speak until Bill was outside with the security man. "This is crazy. I can't believe Bill pulled all this together so fast."

"Well, he was concerned about your safety. I think your dad pulled a few strings as well. There's a panic button under the counter, a camera in the corner, and three others out in the yard. Bill will be able to monitor you from the garage, and your dad has an app on his phone," Jason said, giving her the rundown of the system while Gina sniffed his hand.

Kaitlyn frowned. She felt awkward. "That is way too much. I'm going to feel like a fish in a fishbowl. I don't want to be under scrutiny continuously."

"They just care about you," Jason said as he bent down to pet Gina.

"I understand. But all this is so overwhelming," Kaitlyn stressed, waving her arms around. "I wish people would stop making a deal out of this. Nothing happened. I shouldn't have said anything," Kaitlyn confessed as she shook her head in frustration.

Jason shrugged. He didn't know how to console Kaitlyn and wasn't about to admit he sided with Bill and Rob. He'd had a bad feeling about that guy ever since he tried to push his way into the car and didn't trust him. "What did Simon say to you?" Jason asked, hiding his protective feathers.
"He didn't get a chance and left during the commotion," Kaitlyn replied. "Let's talk about something else. Are we on for the library tonight?"

"Sure, I should be done with work around 5:00 PM, and we can meet for pizza and go from there."

"Sounds good. Now I'd better get to work. I'm trying to get Bill's accounting system moved to a new program. His books are a mess. I'm amazed he could balance his accounts." Kaitlyn giggled.

"Good luck," he said, making fish lips. Then he hurried out the door.

"Very funny." Kaitlyn looked around the room and wondered if someone was watching her. "All I need is you,

Gina girl." Then she applied her thoughts to the new program.

Luckily, her day was busy, which kept her mind off the cameras. Everybody seemed to need things before the weekend, and they wanted them yesterday. Thankfully there had been no sign of Mr. Creepy. At 5:00 PM, Kaitlyn was more than ready to leave. When she got into the car, her heart sank when she heard the song lyrics, *"Darkness has kept the light concealed."*

6) THE MEETING

It's about time you called," the stern voice of an older gentleman bellowed. "You'd better have something good to report." He took a drag from a thick stogy cigar, coated his lungs, and poured an ounce of his faithful friend, Mr. Daniels, into his stained shot glass.

"I was close. It wasn't easy to access, parked in the lot. Too many eyes watching. I'm telling you there's something weird about that car, not normal," replied the cocky young man before he took a pull from a Bud Light and lit up a Marlboro.

"Close is not good enough," the older man yelled as he slammed his fist down on the weathered table. "Haven't I told you boy... only in horseshoes and hand grenades. Were you dealing with either of those?"

"No sir," the younger man replied sarcastically, offering a one finger salute.

"I should've given the assignment to your cousin Brad. I could always count on that boy. You never could do anything right." He then took another drag and blew a smoke ring. As he put his finger through the gray air-design, he broke out into an uncontrollable coughing attack.

"Well, there is still time. I never wanted that stupid job anyway. Give it to Brad," the young man said with a harsh tone. His body was tense, and his fists balled tightly after his father's verbal thrashing. Then a sly smile rescued his mood. "You really should give those things up. They might KILL you someday." Then he himself took a large drag from his cigarette and celebrated with a smoke ring trio.

The old man laughed and in a raspy voice commented, "Not going to give you the pleasure, not quitting. Let's change the subject. I'm going to give you one chance to redeem yourself."

"Oh goody," the younger man said under breath. His cigarette dangled out the side of his mouth as his hands clapped together quietly.

"I mean it boy! No slipups and remember what I told you. Stay back a distance, we don't want them to notice a tail. Then the first chance you get, search the car, and retrieve what I asked for. You understand or do I need to write it all down for you?"

"Yeah, I got it," he replied with a lack of sincerity. "Now are we done here? I do have a life and things to tend too."

"Yes Steven, I believe that's all. Don't disappoint me boy," the older man said.

"I told you not to call me that. My name is Simon."

"Oh yeah, too proud of a punk to want to use your father's name, only a real man deserves that." After the call ended, the older man took a ragged breath, took a puff from his inhaler, and replaced the cell in his hand with the shot of medicine. He rejoiced as the cool liquid slid down his throat. He closed his eyes to embrace the numbing sensation, letting the alcohol release his troubled thoughts. The first burn was always the best; the primer for more to come. His goal, like every night, was to kill the pain and deaden his senses. He wanted to forget about the tormented night, years ago, and the ghost that still haunted his memory.

7) MILEPOST THIRTEEN

Kaitlyn shivered and immediately turned off the radio. The words to the song had chilled her to the bone, and caused unpleasant images to form in her mind. She put aside the thought that Tatiana could harm her. Then she wondered if Tatiana had endured any of those awful things in that song. Feeling sad for her, Kaitlyn touched the console. "Poor girl. I'm going to do everything I can to solve this mystery and bring whoever is responsible to justice. Now, if I only knew where to start," she thought, tossing ideas around in her head.

After pizza, Jason and Kaitlyn opted to walk to the library. It was two blocks away, and the weather was beautiful. There was a light breeze, but that was typical for spring in Oregon.

Electricity hummed up Kaitlyn's arm when Jason took hold of her hand. Half of her wanted to believe it was more for protection than affection. The other half was undecided.

Jason didn't know what had compelled him to reach for Kaitlyn's hand. It just felt right to him. It was a bold move, but he took it as a welcoming sign when she didn't pull away.

The couple walked in silence, both locked in their thoughts. Emotions tugged at their hearts, and yet they were two broken souls too blind to see.

Kaitlyn was relieved when they reached the library and he released hold of her hand. She could breathe normally again. This thing with Jason was happening too fast. She wasn't ready to fall. The problem was she so wanted to. However, the thought of starting a new relationship terrified her.

They took their same spots at the computers as last time and continued looking through the archives. It wasn't long before Kaitlyn came across the article they were looking for. She shrieked before remembering she was in a library, and then instantly covered her mouth.

"What is it?" Jason asked, wondering what had caused the outburst.

Kaitlyn pointed at the computer screen and the newspaper article. "'Lost girl's car found by milepost thirteen near the falls.' I was there the other day. It's where Sunny broke down," Kaitlyn commented, her mind still reeling from the discovery.

"Maybe it's just a coincidence that you ended up there."

"I suppose it could be. Yeah, that's probably what it was," she said, letting the crazy notion go. "You know from now on, after reading this article, I'm going to see that girl's face when I look at the car. How do you think she is connected with it, anyway?"

"Beats me," Jason replied.

"Well, I don't see much more than we already know. I was hoping there would be a clue. Something that would stand out," she commented with a heavy sigh. Kaitlyn looked up at Jason and questioned the alarming look in his eyes. "What's wrong?"

"I just realized something. If I'm not mistaken," Jason answered as he scanned through the archives, "milepost thirteen is also where they found the car when my dad went missing. See," he stressed, "I was right." He tapped his finger on the screen, confirming his find.

Kaitlyn read the article about his father's disappearance. Goosebumps chilled her. She rubbed her arms and tried to concentrate on the material. She could see many similarities between the two incidents. How tragic, she thought.

Jason was reliving a hard part of his past and the pain was etched deep into his face. Stress lines on his forehead told the agonizing story.

"What now?" Jason asked. He looked at her for answers.

"I don't know, but three incidents at the same milepost is not a coincidence. I don't think I ended up there by accident either."

"Then why did you?" Jason challenged her.

"I have no idea. But if I had to guess, I'd say the answer lies somewhere inside that car and at milepost thirteen." Kaitlyn drummed her fingers on the table as she thought about his question. "I have a wild idea, if you're game."

"What's that?"

"Why don't we go up to the falls tomorrow and look around. We can go for a hike and stop at the milepost on our way back. I know Gina would love to get out."

"Sounds like a good plan to me," Jason replied. "Hey, do you think there's a chance my dad is alive?" Jason asked.

Kaitlyn tried to offer a sincere smile. "I don't know. There's always a good chance." Since the two disappearances were similar, she didn't want to mention that he may never be found. But there was no reason to shatter the little hope he had left. And, she thought, maybe by some miracle he was still alive.

"So how does 10:00 AM work for you? That should give us time to play and investigate. I will pack us a lunch," Kaitlyn asked, already looking forward to their date. Then she caught her last thought. Not a date, an assignment!

"That works," Jason replied, his mind lost in thought. "I'd have a better grasp on how to proceed if I knew more about the supernatural, or whatever this is we're dealing with. What if my dad's spirit is stuck inside some vehicle?"

"Oh, that's crazy talk," Kaitlyn replied, waving her hand to dismiss the comment. Only the same thing had also occurred to her. "You know, we are inside a place that contains a vast amount of information. I'm sure somewhere in this library is a section on that topic," she said, opening her arms wide. "Let's go look in the index or ask one of the student librarians."

It turned out there was a large variety of supernatural and other eerie topics, some of which Kaitlyn was not interested in exploring.

"What do we look for?" Jason asked, scanning the area. "There are so many books about spirits, ghosts, vampires, and much more."

Kaitlyn looked around and pondered his question. "I don't know. Your guess is as good as mine. It's not like I'm an expert in this field. Let's just look around and maybe something will jump out at us."

"How about this one?" Jason asked as he showed Kaitlyn a book.

She stared at the picture: a bloody monster on the cover projected an evil presence. "Maybe that one jumped out a little too far. Let's stick to books that have a less dark and demonic nature." Kaitlyn quickly put the book back on the shelf.

After a while, she came across an interesting book. "I don't believe this. I know this person. Only I didn't realize she was a writer."

Jason read the title. "Hmm... 'The Spirit Within by Serena Hallow.' You think there's something in here that will help us?"

Kaitlyn shrugged her shoulders and said, "Don't know. I'm still dealing with the shock of finding out she wrote a book. Which isn't unusual, as she does own a bookstore. Maybe I'll call her. It's been a few months since we talked."

"How do you know her, if you don't mind me asking?"

"We went to college together. Serena is five years my senior. She's my sweet and quirky redheaded friend, and she always found her way into some outlandish predicaments." Kaitlyn laughed. "It will be good to talk with her and find out about this book. Let's add this to the stack. That will give us each three to look at. Hopefully, we can find something. You know," Kaitlyn said, "maybe I'll go see her next weekend. I could use some R&R and girl-time." She pondered the idea for a moment while reading the write-up on the back of the book.

"Ok, I'm game. You name the time," Jason said.

Kaitlyn frowned. "Uh, I don't need a bodyguard, and didn't you hear? ... girl-time! Last time I looked you didn't fit that description unless there's something you'd like to confess." She giggled as she looked him up and down.

"Ha ha," Jason replied, not at all moved by her teasing. "I thought we were a team. After all, it's my dad who's missing. I want to be included in the research and search."

"I don't think it's necessary," she replied. "I promise to report everything I find out."

"I think I should go," Jason pushed.

"I don't want you to go," Kaitlyn stressed.

"Ooh sharp jab," Jason stated. "Do I sense a bit of hostility?"

Kaitlyn shook her head in frustration. "Not hostility, I'm just a little annoyed. This trip will give me time to regroup and put things into perspective."

"So, are you saying I'm annoying?" Jason asked, calling her out.

"That's not what I meant," Kaitlyn said, trying to smooth over her comment, which she now realized had been a thought bubble gone rogue. Using her hands, Kaitlyn described her situation by drawing a square in the air. "I feel like a caged animal. I'm constantly being watched, and I don't like it."

"I'm sorry, Kaitlyn. Yeah, that's probably not much fun. We all mean well, though. I promise I'll step back after the road trip to the coast."

"Really?! Did you hear a word of what I said?" she asked, her irritation growing.

"Kaitlyn, it's for your own good. Don't make me pull rank and talk to Tatiana."

"You wouldn't dare," she exclaimed with a sharpness in her voice and scowling eyes.

Jason was taken back by Kaitlyn's temper. He realized he'd pushed her too far by his last comment. But he didn't want her to go alone, especially when there might be someone threatening her life. "I just think it's a good idea to have someone with you."

"Why the push? No, never mind," she put her hand out. "My dad told you to watch me. You know what? On second thought, I will just call her. And that will solve this debate." She rubbed her hands together to dismiss the subject.

Jason thought Kaitlyn had made the decision fast, and it was probably to appease him. However, he could see right through her façade. He'd let her think she'd won, at least for now.

"You ready to go?" Kaitlyn asked. She felt suffocated and needed to escape before he brought up the trip again. A three-hour road trip with him would be two feet too close for too long.

Saturday morning Kaitlyn dressed in her jeans, sweatshirt, and hiking boots, puttered around the house as she waited for Jason.

Her heart danced in her chest at the sight of him. His jeans hugged his body exactly right, and his t-shirt showed off his muscular biceps. She liked it better when she was blind to his physical physique. This was going to be a long day, she thought. "You drive," Kaitlyn said as she tossed him the keys to Tatiana.

"Sure." He caught them and opened her door. "Let's roll."

With the top down and tunes blasting, the road trip began. Gina, sitting in-between and protected by a seatbelt, embraced the wind in her face. Kaitlyn was lost in her thoughts and was thankful for the radio and road noise. It made it difficult to hold a conversation, which was fine with her. She closed her eyes and found her Zen moment. But the meditation thread was cut short by the sound of Jason's voice.

"Don't be alarmed, but I think we're being followed."

"What do you mean followed?" Kaitlyn asked with a startled look. So much for relaxing, her heartbeat now accelerated. She looked behind to check it out.

"The motorcycle? Are you sure?"

"Almost positive."

Kaitlyn turned back around. "This road is well-traveled. The Falls are one of Oregon's popular tourist attractions. Maybe they're taking advantage of the beautiful weather. It's a perfect day for a drive. Why do you think it's following us?"

Jason glanced in the rearview mirror. He tried to keep a distance ahead of the bike, but still be able to see it. "It's a feeling I have. I didn't want to frighten you, but's it's been tailing us ever since we left town."

"Well, I think you're exaggerating," Kaitlyn speculated.

"Maybe, but at any rate, it's getting closer."

Kaitlyn looked behind her again. She didn't want to believe it and hoped it was a coincidence. "I can't tell who is driving," she reported to Jason.

When she turned to face the front, she noticed all the warning lights lit up on the dash. "What's going on?" Now she was getting scared.

"I don't know," he answered, puzzled by the car's actions.

"This is wild," Kaitlyn commented, as her eyes followed the swishing wipers, adding to the excitement. And not long after that, the flashing lights and door locks joined in on the party. "Why is Tatiana doing this?" Kaitlyn screamed, now in panic mode.

"Maybe she senses danger too!" Jason offered his opinion.

"What are we going to do?"

"I'm going to pull off the road, when it's safe, and let he or she pass us."

"NO!" Kaitlyn yelled. "What if that's what they want. I don't want to become part of the missing persons list. You must have a plan B." She sent him a pleading look.

"There's a little hole-in-the-wall eatery up the road. I'll pull in there."

"Thanks," Kaitlyn said and turned back around to keep a watchful eye on the motorcycle.

Five miles down the road, Jason pulled into the small establishment's driveway and got out of the car.

They watched and prayed the rider would pass by. To their relief, he did, but his wave caused them to quiver.

Jason pulled Kaitlyn close. "Well, since we're here, you want to get a bite?"

Kaitlyn leaned into Jason. She didn't want to admit she felt safe and secure in his arms. Part of her wanted to stay there, but her sensible side took over, and she pulled away. "I guess we can eat the food I brought later. What do they have?"

Jason and Kaitlyn took their burgers and fries order and found a picnic bench under a shade tree. "Do you believe in Sasquatch?" Kaitlyn asked, pointing to the giant poster of Big Foot.

"You know if you'd asked me that a week ago, my answer would've been a definite no. However, now I think anything is possible." He took a bite of his juicy burger and wiped his chin.

"It sure has been a bizarre ride so far, that's for sure," Kaitlyn agreed.

"You still want to continue to the falls? I'd be ok if you'd rather go back after what happened."

"Yes, I still want to go. I'm not going to let some motorcycle rider intimidate me. Let me use the ladies' room, and I'll be ready to go."

"This is such a pretty drive," Kaitlyn expressed, now back on the road. "The Falls in one of my favorite spots in Oregon. Silver Falls Park was established in July 1933," Kaitlyn informed Jason. "However, the story of the area starts back in the early 1800s. The native Americans were the first to settle here. Silver Falls City was platted in 1888 and was located above what is now referred to as the South Falls. It was mostly a small logging community. They had general stores, a hotel, church, dance hall, tavern, and many other buildings."

"Well, aren't you a burst of trivial information. How do you know so much?" Jason inquired.

Kaitlyn shot Jason a friendly smile. "I wrote an essay on it in my writing class in college. It has quite the history. The Trail of Ten Falls loop travels above, behind, and around ten amazing falls. The loop is close to twenty-six miles long. I love to walk behind the South Falls and explore the large caverns. But it's just as stunning to watch above, as the water cascades off the lava-made cliff into a pool 178 feet below. That's enough. I don't want to bore you."

"You're not. I find it all very intriguing," Jason admitted. "Please tell me more."

Kaitlyn cleared her throat. "Ok, you asked for it. In 1935, President Franklin D. Roosevelt deemed it a Recreational Demonstration Area, which started the design and construction of the park's facilities and lodge." Kaitlyn paused a moment to gather her thoughts. "The canyon's history dates to about twenty million years ago when most of Oregon's land was beneath ocean waters."

 "As time went on and millions of years passed, the receding waters and the acts of Mother Nature covered the sandstone left by the ocean with basalt. And time, the winds of change, and erosion created the glorious canyon. People come from all over to take in the beauty of this wonder."

"I can see why," he commented looking around. "Hate to cut my history lesson short but we have arrived."

Jason pulled into a parking spot and before they got out of the vehicle, they made a verbal decision to put the motorcycle incident aside. It was too nice of a day for worrisome thoughts. Besides, there was nothing they could do about it anyway. However, Kaitlyn was glad to see the large crowd of people at the park.

The perfect temperatures had brought out the locals and visitors. As usual, they'd come to picnic and relax in the magical beauty, while the very energetic took on the trails. She felt safer with all the people and wondered if the motorcycle rider was somewhere among them while scoping out the area. If so, they'd never know. She put that disturbing thought behind her. As she glanced around,

Kaitlyn was opened to another wave of emotions. She and Bryan had spent many Saturdays here. So many memories lingered in the park. Around every corner lurked a shadow of her past; a place where they shared a kiss, posed for pictures, or stopped to admire a flower in bloom. The come-alive memories were everywhere. She wished they'd disappear, or at least the pain locked inside them.

Kaitlyn felt Jason take her hand, and she took comfort in his touch. It chased away her sorted past. At least temporarily. She imagined people suspected they were a couple. Kaitlyn wondered that herself. They certainly did portray the image of new love; walking hand in hand, laughing and stealing glances, however, the subject hadn't been brought up or discussed. Why should it, their friendship was new and still quite raw. Besides, she wasn't emotionally prepared to make that leap yet. All the signs were there but neither of them chose to see it.

Jason also fought with ghosts from his past. He remembered all the times he and his dad had hiked the trails, tossed a frisbee in the grass areas, played in the creek and laid on blankets with his parents. Looking out in the field he pictured his mom cuddled next to his dad. They were so happy and in love. He pulled his eyes away and shook off the memory. He missed those days and wished he could go back and hug his dad one more time.

Kaitlyn's touch rescued him from his thoughts and kept him grounded. As much as he hurt, he was going to be in this moment with this sweet girl.

They hiked around the falls, taking pictures and silly selfies. Their conversation stayed light as they focused on their surroundings. Kaitlyn never grew tired of this area. She noticed all the new growth; the wild Calypso Orchids, Corydalis, and Yellow Wood Violets colored the path. And the large Hemlocks shaded the rainforest canyon with a large umbrella, keeping it cooler in some areas. She slipped on her light jacket to ward off a chill, feeling thankful for packing it and being prepared.

Gina amused them with her curious nature, encouraging the couple along as she explored every bush and tree. Even though they'd agreed not to think about the motorcyclist, they were still on alert for anyone that might look the type or acted suspicious. For all they knew, the rider could be walking the trail with them or hiding in the trees watching them. The thought gave Kaitlyn an uneasy feeling. She could tell by Gina's low growl that she also sensed something. It made her mad to feel so vulnerable in these magical surroundings. She didn't like that it threatened her serenity.

After a couple of miles of walking, they decided to turn back. Their fun time was over, and now it was time to investigate.

That was something Kaitlyn wasn't looking forward to doing. She'd be so happy when all this was behind them and she could focus on her normal life again.

When Kaitlyn and Jason returned to the car, they grabbed a snack and some water and shared their pictures. Gina was happy to be back, and after her treat, was ready to ride again.

Minutes later, Jason turned off onto a small pullout. "Why did you come in here?" Kaitlyn questioned Jason's action.

"I didn't, Tatiana did."

"But why here?"

"Look," Jason pointed.

Kaitlyn read the wooden marker. "Ah, milepost thirteen." She shivered and glanced at Jason who had a distant stare. She knew it must be hard for him to go back to his painful past. "I'm sorry," she said and placed her hand on his shoulder. "This has to be rough."

Jason covered her hand with his. "It is," he let out a heavy sigh. "The blow doesn't seem as bad with you here with me," he said with a smile in his eyes.

Kaitlyn could feel the butterflies fluttering in her stomach. His passionate stare was intoxicating, and she just wanted to get drunk on the feeling. Her heart beat wildly as Jason leaned closer. He was going to kiss her. Kaitlyn was helpless, her body melted as she anticipated the touch and taste of his lips.

A loud horn startled the couple and pulled them out of their intimate moment. Kaitlyn bit her bottom lip. "We probably should look around." As she reached for the car door handle, the doors locked. "Quit playing around, Jason."

"Again, I didn't do it."

"I don't understand," Kaitlyn replied. "Why would Tatiana want us here but not let us out of the car?"

Jason tried to lift the lock. "She must sense danger and is trying to protect us."

"Or maybe she is afraid and doesn't want to face her memories. I hope in her current state she isn't able to feel or hurt," Kaitlyn said, her heart hurting for the young girl. Her speculation about Tatiana having feelings was sadly answered, when the engine started rumbling and making a weird sound. "OMG, do you hear that? It sounds like she's crying."

They both jumped when the song lyrics "*I'll be watching you,*" blasted from the radio.

"I don't have a good feeling about this. Tat is trying to warn us. Let's go," Kaitlyn pleaded.

Jason clenched the steering wheel, quiet in thought and popped in a breathmint. "I'm going to check things out. I must find out what happened to my father. You can wait in the car if you like."

Kaitlyn frowned. "And be a sitting duck? I don't think so."

"Oh, a walking duck is so much safer," Jason remarked sarcastically and shut off the engine.

"I'm an Oregonian, born with webbed feet. I'll take my chances." Kaitlyn gave him a fake smile.

"What makes you think she's going to unlock the door?"

Jason shrugged. "I don't know, but I'm going to try and get through her guarded barrier. Tatiana, please let me out. I can take care of myself. I need to do this for both of us. If there is a sliver of a chance there is a clue here, I need to try to find it and you can help by sounding your horn if anyone approaches. You think you can do that?"

Tatiana tooted her horn twice and unlocked the doors.

"Thank you. We shouldn't be too long," Jason commented. Before he exited the vehicle, he pulled out a handgun from the glovebox. Noticing an alarming look on Kaitlyn's face as she stared at the pistol, he immediately spoke up to put her mind at ease. "Before you say anything, yes, I have a permit for this Smith & Wesson 9 mm, and yes, I know how to shoot it. My dad took me shooting in the mountains at a young age, and I go to the rifle range several times a year."

"They just make me nervous," Kaitlyn admitted. "However, I'm glad you have it. If there's any trouble, these ducks are going to be prepared." She chuckled at her pun. It was the only way to keep her sanity. "You stay here," she instructed Gina before exiting the vehicle.

They found a narrow path. Jason led the way, his hand keeping a tight grasp on Kaitlyn's. After traveling a few hundred yards, the trail opened into a large grassy area.

Kaitlyn admired a small hill covered in wildflowers. Under different circumstances, she'd stop and catch the beauty on her cell phone. But right now, all she wanted to do was get done with this investigation and lock herself in the car.

They continued until the path reached a dead-end, that was unless you wanted to follow another trail over a steep embankment.

Kaitlyn looked over the side and hoped that wasn't Jason's plan. "Now what?" she asked.

"I don't know," Jason replied as he raked his fingers through his hair. "There's no way we can go down there. We don't have the right equipment with us." He stepped close to the edge, and inside the brush, off to the side, he saw a colorful object stuck to a tree branch. He held onto a limb, then stretched to his limit, and plucked it from the tree branch.

"What is it?" Kaitlyn asked, her curiosity pulling her closer.

"It's a piece of material, like someone's flannel shirt." Jason froze. "I think it's my dad's. I'm sure of it. I gave him one just like this on Christmas the year before he went missing."

Kaitlyn examined the cloth. "Why didn't the police find it? How is it still there?"

"Hmm..." Jason pondered her questions. " It's possible the authorities missed it, or maybe it was stuck, and the wind moved it to that location. Of course, those are just speculations. Is it possible my dad fell down there?" Jason shuddered at the thought.

"Let's hope not, that would be a pretty brutal fall."

"I still don't know why he was here," Jason commented. "Let's look around this area. Maybe there are more clues."

Their time was cut short when the alarming sound of Tatiana's horn blared.

8) ROAD TRIP

"What's going on?" Kaitlyn asked, her face locked in fear.

"I don't know," Jason answered as he pulled out his gun. "Stay close behind me."

They made it back to the car in time to see the taillight of a motorcycle spewing a trail of gravel in its wake.

"Look out," Jason said, pushing Kaitlyn out of the line of flying tiny rocks. This move caused him to land on top of her and the gun to slip out of his hand.

Every nerve ignited in her as she laid frozen on the ground. She couldn't decide if it was the shock of the fall or the hard body pressed against hers that prevented her from moving. She wasn't in a hurry to get up, so instead she listened to the rhythm of her shallow breaths as they matched Jason's heartbeat pulsating on her chest. Kaitlyn then made the mistake of gazing into his intoxicating stare, causing her to melt under the fiery look in his ice blue eyes. Lost in the moment, she licked her dry lips.

Jason gazed down at the beauty staring up at him. He couldn't resist the sight of the glistening lips that pulled him closer. His only thought was how bad he wanted to kiss her.

Kaitlyn's body trembled from the heat of Jason's breath warming her cheek. She could almost taste the lingering scent of mint when his lips lightly brushed hers. She longed for him to pull her into his arms and kiss her more deeply. But just when her lips parted to invite him in, Tatiana sounded her horn and broke the blissful moment.

Jason jumped up, and, after shaking off the effects of his sensual coma, he helped Kaitlyn up and escorted her to the car. He was relieved by the interruption. A relationship was the furthest thing from his mind. At least that's what he kept telling himself. However, that might pose a challenge after being so close to her.

Now every time he looked at her, he'd wonder what it would be like to crush those delectable lips with his.

But right now, he needed to focus on finding his dad and not be swayed by a sweet redheaded distraction. He picked up the gun, got in the car, and handed it to Kaitlyn. "Please put this in the glovebox," he requested. "Then hold on. I'm going to try and catch up with the motorcycle, though it's probably a longshot. He's probably miles away by now. Let's see what this baby can do."

Kaitlyn carefully took the gun and put it safely away, and then grabbed hold of the seat. "Be careful; you're carrying special cargo."

"Don't worry, I wouldn't let anything happen to this girl," he said as he smirked and patted the dashboard.

"Really!" Kaitlyn exclaimed with a dramatic eye roll.

Three miles down the road, Jason finally let up on the gas. "Seems like he's given us the slip. He could be hiding in any of the many pullouts," he commented as he perused the side of the road.

"Bummer," Kaitlyn replied. She tried to sound sincere, but underneath she was relieved. Not seeing him again would be ok with her.

It was almost dusk when Jason pulled into her driveway. Kaitlyn had dozed off half-way back and rubbed her tired eyes. "Must've been all the excitement. I usually don't fall asleep that easy."

"I'm beat myself," he confessed during a yawn. "It's been a long day, but I had a good time."

"Yeah, me too," Kaitlyn said, looking away from his warm eyes as she stepped out of the car and walked toward him.

"I'd better go," Jason said. He looked down and kicked a small stone.

"See you Monday," Kaitlyn said with a wave.

Jason looked up and was drawn in by Kaitlyn's smile. Without thinking, he pulled her into his arms, gently placed a kiss on her forehead, and then walked quickly to his truck.

Kaitlyn had gasped when he embraced her. She hadn't expected the kiss and gave a deep sigh as she rubbed her forehead.

Jason climbed into his truck. He was impressed with his self-control, only he had wanted to direct the kiss to those sweet lips. Shaking off the thought, he turned on the engine, settled in, and headed home.

Kaitlyn spent Sunday catching up on house chores and laundry. She called Serena to confirm she'd be around the next weekend. She ended the day eating leftovers she got from her mom and taking a long walk with Gina.

The following week treated her well. There were no spine-chilling events that took place and no sign of her creepy stalker. Kaitlyn had settled into her position at the garage with self-confidence, and she found she was even able to resolve most problems and find her own mistakes.

When Friday rolled around, Kaitlyn was exhausted. It had been an adjustment balancing her time with both jobs. She figured it would take a couple of weeks until she fell into a routine. Tatiana had been on her best behavior, and Jason hadn't been around much because of his busy schedule. She did feel a prickle of guilt for not telling him that she was going to Astoria without him. It wasn't like she had to answer to him; however, his dad's disappearance led to her decision to make the trip. She should've included him but felt she needed some "me" time, and he'd only be a distraction, a handsome distraction. Her body tingled as she remembered their near kiss at Milepost 13.

Kaitlyn planned to call him when she was out of town. "Chicken," she mumbled to herself, pushing the thought out of her head. She ate a light meal and finished packing her bag. Then prepared a tub with all of Gina's necessities and took care of any last-minute details. At 10:00, she turned out the light, set her alarm for seven, and crawled into bed. Within minutes she was asleep, Gina's head under her arm.

The following day Kaitlyn was up with the birds. She wanted some time to reflect, regroup, and analyze, for there were more than enough crazy-making thoughts swirling in her head. The last few weeks Kaitlyn had felt as though she'd been living someone else's life. Ever since encountering Tatiana, her world had gone three kinds of sideways, which left her unsettled. It was as though someone had plucked her from a normal, stable life and cast her in a missing person's mystery, co-starring a car with a childish behavior.

And because of Jason her emotions were running on overdrive, and that was a road she wasn't ready to drive down. The trip to the coast would help shake him loose from her head and hopefully bring her back to her senses.

Kaitlyn filled her travel mug with coffee and took Gina for a walk. Upon returning, she was perturbed by the sight of Jason standing by the car with an overnight bag by his feet. She set the cup down, folded her arms at her chest and gave him a perplexed look. She asked, "What are you doing here?"

"It looks like you're going somewhere," he replied smugly, checking out the loaded car.

"Maybe, but it's really none of your business," she replied with a displeased look.

Jason rubbed the top of the car. "Oh, but I think it is. I know your plans for the coast, and I'm a little upset you didn't tell me."

Kaitlyn blew out a breath. "Look, Jason, it has nothing to do with you. I just need some time by myself to think and hang out with my friend. I promise I'll give you a full report when I get back."

"Sorry, but no can do. I promised your dad I'd go with you," Jason stated.

Kaitlyn folded her arms at her chest. "Well, you can tell my dad that I don't need a babysitter."

"Listen, Kaitlyn," Jason said, his hand on her arm. "We are both concerned about you, especially with this guy stalking you. What happens if he follows you? Besides, I'm invested in this trip as much as or maybe more than you are. After all, this is about my dad."

Kaitlyn pulled her arm away while she thought about his comment. "Fine!" she replied sharply. He'd got her with the dad-card and his sad eyes. She had *to* be a sucker when it came to family and teary, dreamy eyes. "You'll have to fight Gina for shotgun, and it looks like she's already beaten you to it." Kaitlyn laughed but then changed her tune when she realized that meant he'd be seated next to her.

Jason stared at the content dog proudly owning her seat and could've sworn there was a smile on her face. "No problem, I'll get to sit closer to you." Jason climbed in and got settled.

Arrgh," Kaitlyn growled under her breath. "Let me lock up, and I'll be right out." She was frustrated with this situation and was still fuming when she got into the car. It was going to be impossible to keep from touching him. Her dad was undoubtedly going to hear about this setup.

"Hope you don't mind," Jason said, "but I wrote down a few notes and mapped out the fastest route. Also, there's a great restaurant along the way."

Kaitlyn tried to keep her temper at bay as she bit her lip. "First of all, you can put your notes away; I know how to get there. Also, we're going to my favorite place to eat." She flashed him a Pan Am smile, started Tatiana, and headed up the road.

Jason glanced out the window when Kaitlyn stopped outside her parent's house. "Why are we stopping here?" he asked.

"I'd like to say to drop you off," she answered with a sly smile as they walked up to the porch.
"Saturday mornings, we always have family brunch at my parents. I've called ahead to warn them of your arrival, but since you and my dad are best buds, they probably already have a place set for you." Joy, joy, Kaitlyn thought. She wasn't looking forward to this at all. The word awkward crossed her mind more than once. "Be prepared for a crazy adventure, as my family can be overwhelming at

times," Kaitlyn said as she opened the door to the sound of laughter.

After the meet and greet, Jena walked with Kaitlyn to the table and hip-bumped her, followed by a wink. Kaitlyn rolled her eyes and, before taking her seat, hunted down her dad in the den.
"Dad, what were you thinking asking Jason to go with me? I don't need a bodyguard. I've done this trip many times, and Gina will protect me."

"Hi dear," he said as he looked up from his computer. "Your mom and I thought it was best, especially after the motorcycle incident," Bob admitted.

Kaitlyn raked her fingers through her short hair, her frustration growing. "He told you about that. He had no right. I can't believe the two of you." She lifted her arms in the air.

Bob put his arms on his daughter's shoulders and looked her in the eyes. "Honey, it's for your own good. What harm is it to have him ride along? He's a nice guy. Besides, your mom and I would rest easy knowing you're not on the road alone, at least until they find this guy who's stalking you. Please...?" he asked with pleading eyes.

Kaitlyn sighed. "I already told him he could go, but I just wanted to let you know I'm not at all pleased about it. It also looks like I'm outnumbered, so there's no use in taking this discussion any further. Could you do me a favor? Next time talk to me first before you rearrange my life." She hugged her dad and took his arm as he escorted her down the hall.

Bob looked down at Kaitlyn and whispered, "I will try, but if it puts your life in jeopardy, there is no bargaining."

When they entered the dining room, they took their seats. Of course, Jason was seated next to her.
Inside she shuddered. Could this day get any worse? At least Carson was on Jason's other side and was posing many questions his way. However, she'd forgotten how bold he could be - out of the mouths of babes. Kaitlyn almost choked when Carson asked if he was going to marry her and have babies. "No..." Kaitlyn stated firmly, clearing that thought from any curious minds that had been listening. "Jason is just a friend. Now eat those pancakes before they get cold." She took another large bite of hers and, even though they were drenched in syrup, the cakes were hard to swallow. She wasn't at all hungry, and the large lump stuck in her nervous stomach. It also disturbed her that he fitted into the scene so well, not as a guest, but as family.

After breakfast, Kaitlyn helped to clean up and tried to avoid answering any questions about her guest.
Jason had disappeared with her dad, and she could only imagine they were talking about poor defenseless Kaitlyn. The thought made her blood boil. Well, it wasn't going ruin her weekend. Kaitlyn then pondered the situation and thought she'd been a little hard on Jason. After all, he was only looking out for her safety and was hoping to find answers to his father's disappearance. There was nothing wrong with his intentions. It was the thought of him being so close to her and wondering what it would be like to kiss him that bothered her. The trip to the ocean was going to be a long drive, she thought.
When they returned to the car, Kaitlyn opened the passenger door and called Gina in. "You can ride shotgun for a while. Gina said it was ok." Then she climbed into

the car. Even with him seated on the other side., Kaitlyn felt it was still too close.

"I appreciate it, but I was perfectly fine where I was," Jason said as he settled in the passenger seat.

Before Kaitlyn backed out of her parent's drive, she turned to Jason. "Look, I'm sorry about the way I acted. Your appearance at my house took me by surprise, and I don't like it when someone else is trying to control my life. You were just being nice, and you're right. I should've included you. I know how much you want to find your dad."

"What?" Jason exclaimed. "You said I was right?"

"Really!" Kaitlyn screeched, "that's all you got out of my apology?"

"What can I say? Men are fairly simple," he stated nonchalantly.

"Uh-huh yeah, simple," Kaitlyn said as she shook her head. "So, what all did you have in your notes? I could be swayed to take another route."

"Yours is good! I think we are going to get along fine on this road trip," Jason admitted. Then he leaned back, stretched his legs, and pulled his ball cap over his eyes.

Oh lordy, Kaitlyn thought, her eyes glued on the sexy, relaxed man two feet away.

Jason lifted one side of his hat, catching Kaitlyn in her trance. "Are we going to go?" he said with a wink.

"Uh, sure," Kaitlyn replied, her face red after being caught. OMG, I hope I wasn't drooling, she thought, touching her chin, and starting their journey.

Kaitlyn had decided her worrying had been for nothing. She enjoyed Jason's company and was happy he'd come along with her. At the half-way point, they stopped at a state park to let Gina out and stretch. They walked down to a little creek hidden by a patch of trees. She'd done great in the car but being out here in the woods alone with Jason left her feeling vulnerable. Her emotions were twisted like the branches on the corkscrew willow next to the water. All she had to do was look at Jason to see he was feeling something too. Before she could back away, he pulled her into his arms and found her lips. She melted in his embrace and surrendered to the moment.

The sound of Gina's bark pulled the couple from their intimate state. A young couple was walking on the path, and Gina was alerting them of their presence. "We probably should get back on the road," Jason commented.

"Hmm..." Kaitlyn said, starry-eyed as she touched her lips. "Oh yeah," she stated after realizing her reaction.

Jason took her hand and led her back to the car. Their unspoken silence told the story and held their thoughts and secrets.

When Kaitlyn started the engine, she jumped in her seat. Another song vibrated the speakers as it played at full volume. She immediately lowered the sound, and they both listened to the words, *"Ring of Fire."* Then the radio switched back to the current station.
"Wow, she's never changed the radio station before," Kaitlyn stated in amazement. "And what a strange choice

of words. Crazy car, I wish I knew what all that means," Kaitlyn commented, grateful they'd moved onto another topic, leaving the kiss by the riverbank for the time being.

"Hmm..." Jason contemplated the question for a second. "It's obvious she's sending us messages through musical clues. Let's put all the songs in sequence and see if we can come up with the meaning or connection."

"Great idea," Kaitlyn agreed as she dug in her purse for a tablet and pen. "Let's see, I can't remember them in the correct order, but I think between the two of us, we can come up with them all. The first one mentioned *'Country Roads.'* Can we assume that whatever happened was in the country? Given where we've been, I'd say it was off Silver Falls Highway, at or near milepost thirteen."

"I'll go with that," Jason commented. "Next is *'Everybody's Crazy About a Sharp Dressed Man.'* You think the guy that hurt her wore a suit, maybe a businessman?"

"Hmm..." Kaitlyn sighed. "We'll put that down as a possibility," and she made notes about the song. "Moving on," she said, going down the list. "'*Sharp Knife of a Short Life'* doesn't sound good. Do you think someone stabbed her?" Kaitlyn asked, her heart sad for the young girl as she patted the door to offer Tatiana comfort.

"I don't know," Jason replied, also pausing a moment to consider the possibility. "The next one is just as bad; *'Come on, Pretty Baby, Kiss me Deadly.'*"

Kaitlyn felt a shiver down her spine. "I just don't want to imagine what that could mean. Let's move on to the next, which I'd say isn't much better. *'Darkness Kept the Light*

Concealed.' I'll put an asterisk by the creepy songs, and we'll revisit them when we have more info."

"Good Idea. This may be a shot in the dark, but maybe she was poisoned and buried alive with a blindfold or put in some dark place," Jason said, tossing out an idea.

"God, I hope not," Kaitlyn said as she almost felt the pain radiating through the car and moved quickly onto the next song. "'*School's Out Forever'* could signify it happened after school was out for the summer."

Jason nodded. "I can go along with that. And '*I'll be Watching You.'* She knew someone was watching, and it was an attempt to warn us?"

Kaitlyn shivered at the thought. "Last but certainly not least, the strange one tonight: '*Ring of Fire.*'"

Jason shrugged, "I'm at a loss with that one as well. So, let's just say we're right about most of these clues. I still don't know how it applies to my dad's disappearance," Jason commented in frustration.

Kaitlyn shot a glance at Jason and could see the desperation in his hollow stare. It pained her to witness his raw emotion, and there wasn't anything in her power she could do to eliminate the hurt. But she could try and divert it by offering some hope. "Hey, we're making progress. It's gradual, but we can celebrate tiny breakthroughs and small wins. It's more than likely your dad was following the same trail and figured it out, which might have led to his disappearance. The sooner we pull all the clues together, the closer we'll get to the answer. So please stay with me."

Jason sat with alertness in his eyes and let out a heavy sigh. "I wanted the answers yesterday. It's been so hard on mom and me not knowing what happened. It's like reading a book and never reaching the end. There's no closure; no last page." He paused and stared out the window.

"I don't know if it would make it easier knowing what happened because we won't be able to change the past, but it would bring a sense of peace in our hearts. Depending on the outcome, either the grieving can begin, or the celebration can commence. The not knowing eats you inside." Jason turned his attention back to Kaitlyn. "I try not to dwell on it, but his eyes stare back at me every time I look in the mirror. I can try to stay focused, but I can't make any promises."

Kaitlyn threw him a smile. "I understand. Maybe Tatiana will open up with Serena." She pointed to a sign designating the mileage. "It looks like we'll be there soon."

Twenty minutes later, Jason parked in front of Books on the Corner. "Serena doesn't get off until 4:30 today. She said Cliff is going to stop by and rescue you from our devilish clutches," she teased giving an evil sounding chuckle.

Jason smirked as he followed Kaitlyn through the door. "I like the guy already."

Kaitlyn stepped into the bookstore and was immediately drawn in by the smell of freshly brewed coffee. Her eyes cruised the store, looking for her friend. "I don't see Serena. Let's get some coffee while we wait." Neither of them noticed the stranger lurking outside. Hidden by the shadow of a tall oak tree, he stood peering through the window.

Linda K. Richison

9) TRIP TO ASTORIA

Kaitlyn took in the layout as she walked through the shop. She noticed that Serena had made a few minor changes since her last visit, but for the most part, the store was how she'd remembered it. Close to the door, a display shelf proudly held the most popular books. Large shelves lined the aisles creating maze-like rows that were home to a large variety of publications. Next to the cash register, on the counter, stood a glass case of jewelry for sale—each piece tagged with the name of a local artist. A sofa covered in pillows and a box of toys designated the children's area in the far corner. Kaitlyn smiled as she remembered the glazed look in the children's eyes when she'd filled in for Storytime last summer.

Jason took hold of Kaitlyn's arm while he checked out the place. "It just looks like a regular bookstore. Where do you think this James character in her book hangs out?" he asked, his curious eyes searching the area.

Kaitlyn stopped, turned to Jason with a peculiar look, and answered, "Of course, it looks normal. I should've never let you read that book. There's no reason to worry. James was a spirit friend of Serena's, and I'm sure he's moved on."

"Yeah, I know that's what the book said. But it still makes you wonder."

Kaitlyn offered a reassuring smile. "I think it's safe to assume he's not here. However, Serena is hanging around here somewhere. From the aroma of the sweet coffee beans, I'd say she's in the bistro."

"Lead the way," Jason said, motioning Kaitlyn ahead with a sweep of his arm.

They found Serena behind the counter, preparing a specialty coffee for a customer. She looked up and offered the couple a wide smile. "Hi guys, go ahead and choose a drink, and I'll get to it after I finish up here." After she swirled a heart design in the coffee, she handed it to a gentleman, took his payment, and wished him a good day.

"Wow, it seems like everyone wanted coffee at the same time," she laughed, then brushed a strand of wild red hair from her eyes.

"It's so good to see you, girlfriend," Kaitlyn said, stepping up to the counter. "This is Jason."

After the meet and greet, Kaitlyn and Jason found a table and waited for their order. Kaitlyn took a seat across from him and glanced around.

"I can't believe how much this place has changed. When Serena first moved into the apartment upstairs, this coffee area was much smaller. I see Cliff has knocked out a couple of walls and extended the coffee bar and made room for more tables."

"It looks good," Jason replied with a nod, then looked up at Serena, who had arrived at their table.

Serena served them their coffees and pulled up a chair from a nearby table. "I have a couple of minutes to chat before another customer comes in craving a coffee. It's almost three, and that seems to be the time people need a caffeine fix. Cliff should be here in about fifteen minutes. He's giving a bid on a job just down the road. He said to tell you, Jason, that he won't' leave you with the cackling hens too long." Serena shook her head. "He's such a funny man." She looked up and noticed a customer awaiting their java fix and excused herself. "Kait, I'm off at four. We can go to happy hour downtown on the pier, and the guys can meet us for dinner at six. That should give us girls time to catch up and talk about these yahoos in our life." She directed her last comment to Jason and walked away.

Jason smirked. "I can see how you two can be friends. You both have that witty humor."

Kaitlyn raised her brows as she looked at him over her coffee cup. "Yep, I guess you could say we're not afraid to speak our minds." She pointed her finger at Jason. "And no comments from the peanut gallery."

Jason raised his hands in front of his chest. "I plead the fifth."

Serena was able to get away after the short stream of people. "That should be it for a while. However, I might see a few loners coming in after work."

Kaitlyn watched with a stoic expression, smiling inside, as Cliff came up behind his wife.

"Oh," Serena said with a jump. For a moment, her eyes held a startled look, but as she turned her head, they softened as she received a kiss in greeting from her husband, then she teasingly swatted him away. "Where are your manners?" she voiced with red blushing cheeks.

Cliff gave a flirtatious grin and whispered in her ear, "Well, if you weren't so irresistible, I could keep my manners intact."

Serena stepped away and brought her attention back to her guests. "Cliff, this is Jason, and you know Kaitlyn."

Cliff hugged Kaitlyn then held out his hand to Jason. "Sorry, man, I planned on being here sooner, but the bid took longer than expected. Hope these two haven't driven you to drink," he said, with a smart aleck grin.

Jason shook his firm grip, matching it. "Only strong coffee. Holding my own." Then he turned his head to avoid the fake smile Kaitlyn had delivered.

"So, you ready to go? We can go hang at the house, grab a beer, maybe catch a game on the tube, and meet the ladies for dinner later."

"I'm down," Jason replied, then surprised Kaitlyn with a stolen kiss good-bye.

"Hey Jason," she called out. "Please take Gina with you. She'd loved to see Brody, her playmate."

"Got it," he replied.

After Cliff and Jason left, Serena joined Kaitlyn at the table. "I've some cleaning up to take care of, and then we can go. Becky should be back any minute. She had to take her twin boys to get their shots." Serena winced. "Been there done that, and it's not a fun time. Anyway, she graciously offered to stay till closing and do the books. I don't know what I'd do without my cousin; she's been a Godsend for sure."

"How are your babies doing?" Kaitlyn asked. "I'm excited to see what you two beautiful people have created."

"I'm afraid you'll have to wait. Mom and Dad stole them for the weekend. It's a nice break, and it gives us more time to visit. They're both growing like weeds and quite a handful, but I'd never change being a mom to those precious small humans." She giggled. "Lyla May is two and was gifted, or maybe cursed, with my wild red hair. She screams when I try to brush it. She has a temper and never misses a chance to tease her older brother. And between you and me, I think she can sense things too."

"Oh no," Kaitlyn replied, covering her smirk.

"Alex James, AJ for short, is four. He has long curly hair that his dad won't let me cut. He loves to pick on his sister. He reminds me of a miniature Cliff and is following in his footsteps as he is always building something." Serena pulled out her phone and showed Kaitlyn pictures of her kids.

"They are such cute little darlings. You guys did well.   I can't wait to see them next time I visit."

Serena gave a proud mom smile and set her phone down. "So, what's the story with you and Jason?" She leaned in to get the scoop.

"There isn't any. We're just friends," Kaitlyn answered, hiding the truth.

"Uh-huh, not buying it. I don't think friends kiss on the lips, and the look in his eyes holds more than a mere friendship. I can see the glow on your face. Come on, spill it, girlfriend."

Kaitlyn let out a heavy sigh. It was always hard to hide anything from her friend. She was going to have to work on her poker face. "Well, we might have kissed, and yes, I may be a little attracted to him. But we are not on the same page. There's a silent agreement that neither of us is looking for a relationship. Besides, I'm not sure if he's right for me. I don't want to make another mistake."

Serena placed her hand over Kaitlyn's. "What makes a guy right for you? What are you looking for?"

Kaitlyn cupped her hands around her coffee as she pondered the thought. "I just want a man that looks at me the way Cliff looks at you, with the fiery passion and love in his eyes. I want to be his first thought in the morning and his last thought before he ends the day. He needs to be honest, sincere, and get me, then everything else will fall into place."

"Well, I believe Jason checks all the boxes. Even if you are too blind to see, I can tell he adores you."

Kaitlyn tilted her head and asked, "How do you know? You have an insight into relationships too?"

Serena chuckled. "Not exactly. I can read the signs and feel the chemistry. I was in the same place you were when I came here. I was scared and wasn't ready for a relationship, but Cliff kept pushing. James, the spirit who used to occupy the shop, would say to me, 'Those sparks between you and that young man are so hot they could fry my elements.' I didn't believe him and was in denial. James was intuitive and seemed to have an insight into people's spirits," Serena said as she looked up as though he was still nearby.

Kaitlyn gave an endearing smile. "You miss him?"

Serena nodded. "Sometimes, I try not to think about him much, or I become an emotional mess. The point I want to make is never let love slip through your hands. I'm so glad Cliff didn't give up on me. That's enough about my life. Help me clean up, and you can tell me about this car of yours."

Kaitlyn followed Serena to the coffee bar and started in on the dishes.

"So, what's her name again?" Serena asked as she wiped down the counter.

"Tatiana. There's nothing more I can think of that I haven't already told you on the phone.

Do you think there's a chance you can get through to her?"

Serena shook her head full of long raging curls. "Beats me. It depends on what earthly plane she resides in. If she is as broken as you say, there's a strong possibility she won't let me break through her protective barrier of steel. I'm going to have to gain her trust, and that'll be a challenge since she doesn't know me."

Kaitlyn tilted her head to the side. "I still can't believe all this. It's so crazy and surreal and so hard to grasp a hold on. How did you ever do it? How'd you know you had the power?"

"I don't know," Serena answered with a shoulder shrug. "It just happened. James and I became terrific friends, and he taught me so much."

Kaitlyn washed the dishes in the sink. "I don't think friendship is possible. Tatiana dislikes me and hasn't been afraid to show it."

"Well, after I clean the coffee machine, you can introduce me to this young spirit, and I'll see what I can find out. I make no promises, though." Serena chuckled.

A loud noise coming from the book area startled the women and ended their conversation. They came running out to see what had caused the crashing sound and discovered a book display lying on its side. Books lay scattered around the broken pieces of wood.

 Kaitlyn caught an image as it dashed past the window. She rushed over to check it out.

"Who do you think did this?" Serena asked in bewilderment, stepping over the mess to join Kaitlyn.

"I don't know." But the rumble of a motorcycle racing by answered that question. "Oh no," Kaitlyn gasped.

"What?" Serena asked her scared friend.

"That's the motorcycle guy I was telling you about, that is stalking me. He must've followed us here, and look," Kaitlyn pointed to her car. "I think Tatiana senses him too. Her lights are flashing." She pulled her glazed eyes away from the street. "Please do me a favor and don't mention this to Jason. He'll just get worried and want to stick like glue to my side. And I tell you, I'm so tired of being under the scrutiny of a watchful eye."

"You've got my word, but you might think about telling him. That guy might be dangerous."

"Maybe, but let's not tell him right away. Let's just try and have a fun normal evening. This week has been a total nightmare. I might even have a drink or two."

Serena laughed. "Ok, let's go look at your car so we can get our party started. We'll have the guys be the designated drivers tonight."

Kaitlyn studied Serena as she inspected Tatiana. It was like watching a doctor examining a patient. She slowly moved around the car, her hand gently trailing down the metal. Every few feet, she'd lean her head down on the vehicle. Kaitlyn compared it to the doctor listening for a heartbeat or searching for a pulse. Viewing it from that perspective made it easier for her to grasp. After ten minutes, Kaitlyn asked, "Has she divulged any wild secrets?"

Serena shook her head. "Nope, the young thing is tight bumpered," she giggled at her pun and made-up word. "I can sense a deep shyness."

"HA!" Kaitlyn exclaimed. "Tatiana is many things, but shy is not one of them."

Serena ignored Kaitlyn's sarcasm, opened the car door, and stuck her head inside. "She's probably hiding her fear with shyness. I don't blame her. After her scare tonight and given that she doesn't know me, I'm probably not going to get through. I must gain her trust. Then maybe I can read her vibes." Serena closed the door and gave her full attention to Kaitlyn. "That's only speculation. My experience dealing with spirits in automobiles is zero," Serena said, making the symbol with her fingers.

Kaitlyn blew out a heavy sigh and leaned her arm against the car. "So, what do we do now? I was hoping you'd be able to find out something."

"Tomorrow I'll take her out for a short drive, try to gain her confidence, and maybe she'll open up. No guarantees, though. Here, toss me the keys. I'm dying to get behind the wheel."

Kaitlyn let out an exasperated sigh, when the car started for Serena. "What a brat," she said quietly.

"She drives smooth, such a sweet girl," Serena patted the console to establish a bond.

"Yeah, right - sweet."

Serena threw her friend a displeased look. "You're not helping here."

"Sorry," she halfway apologized. "It just frustrates me that I have to threaten her to get her to behave. With everyone else, she's Miss Polly perfect. Why is that?"

Serena bit her bottom lip. "I'd say she feels most comfortable with you and can be her true self. From what you've told me, she's been trapped here for a while. This little spirit is getting antsy. Am I right, Tat?"

At first, there was no response, then the car lights on the dash flashed on and off.

"Guess that's her way of communicating," Serena surmised.

"Yep, through all her operational parts. And for her, that response was quite mellow. She also sends messages through lyrics in various songs."

With that comment said, a song exploded from the radio.

This rattled Kaitlyn's nerves, which were still very fragile from the motorcycle incident.   Maybe her two drinks would turn into three of four. She seldom drank to get drunk, only relax. This time she was going to make an exception.

Kaitlyn immediately turned the loud noise off. She wasn't in the mood for another song, especially one with a list of random numbers and some girl named Jenny. It made no sense to her. They hadn't been able to tie all the other songs together yet. If it were necessary, she had faith Tatiana would play it again.

Serena threw a glance at her frightened friend. "Another song?"

"Yes," Kaitlyn answered, "but I don't feel like dealing with it tonight. I'm going to pretend that none of this has happened and live-in denial for just for a few hours." She giggled hysterically and looked out the window.

"Fair enough," Serena agreed.

After they arrived at the restaurant and two white Zinfandels were flowing through her veins, Kaitlyn was finally in a relaxed state of mind and was feeling no pain. One half-glass more, a cruise down memory lane, and some tears and laughter later, her face lit up when Jason appeared at the table. "Hi guys," Kaitlyn greeted the men excitedly.

Noticing the sparkle in Jason's and Kaitlyn's eyes, Serena stood up and immediately took hold of her husband's arm. "Excuse us. I want to show Cliff the Goonies apparel. The kids need new t-shirts."

"What? We just got here, and we just bought them each one last month," Cliff commented, giving his wife a strange look, and then giving Jason and Kaitlyn a shoulder shrug.

Serena put on her winning loving smile and pulled him away from the table. "Maybe they have new ones."

"They are so cute together, aren't they?" Kaitlyn commented.

"I guess," Jason said, not knowing how to respond. "Cliff seems like a cool guy."

"They are the bestest, I mean best," Kaitlyn said, quickly covering her slurred bunder. "I might've had just a teeny-weeny bit more alcohol than I'm used to," she admitted, her fingers gapped apart, displaying the amount. "It's been a crazy week. Heck, it's been a crazy ride ever since I found that car. She's been nothing but trouble. But then again, I never would've met you," she admitted with dreamy eyes.

"You mean the annoying thorn in your side," he said teasingly before he gave the waitress his order.

"I never said that. But I do have to confess that you are a very handsome annoyance," Kaitlyn giggled.

Jason wasn't sure how to react to Kaitlyn's confession. It was apparent that the alcohol was acting as liquid courage, allowing her to speak her mind. He admitted to himself that there might be feelings on his side towards her, but was he ready for a relationship? He had jumped back and forth with this idea ever since they'd almost kissed at the milepost, and he was utterly torn after the kiss today at the river.

His tug-of-war emotions were making it hard to commit, one way or the other. He so wanted to feel her soft skin and kiss such inviting lips. Maybe he was putting too much thought into this and should let the evening progress and see where it took them.

"Are you there?" Kaitlyn asked, waving her hands in front of his face to get his attention.

"Uh, yes, just thinking."

Kaitlyn took another sip of wine, another drop for courage. "I'm the one drinking, and you go into a blackout." Kaitlyn laughed at her joke. She took another sip of wine. "So, I have something to tell you, and you have to promise not to overreact, or I won't tell you," she said with a serious demeanor.

"I promise," Jason replied, holding up his hand like he was pledging an oath.

She leaned in closer than necessary as if to expose a secret, then Kaitlyn revealed her truth. "I'm pretty sure Simon followed us."

"Why do you think that?" Jason asked with baited curiosity.

Kaitlyn placed her elbows on the table and rested her head in her hands. She searched the restaurant for prying ears or seeking eyes. When she felt it was safe, she told him, "He was in the bookstore spying on me. The loud crash of a book display he'd knocked over had him scurrying out the door like a little busted rat. Serena and I watched as he flew by her window on his motorcycle. Yep, he left on his rat mobile." She giggled, then caught herself as her head slipped out of her hands. "Whoops."

Jason folded his arms over his chest and leaned the chair back. He crossed his legs and commented, "I see."

"You can just wipe that smug look off your face, mister. As you can see, I'm safe and sound, and I don't need you to guard this body," she teased, running her hand down her side.

Jason gave a sly grin at Kaitlyn's alcohol-induced slip and decided not to reply because his thoughts traveled down a dark road as they followed her hand. He watched Kaitlyn as she blew a stray strand of curly hair out of her eyes. He had to admit she was beautiful and alluringly sexy in her relaxed state. It was hard not to want to pull her into his arms and devour her intoxicated lips dripping with the sweet taste of grapes. However, there were other more severe matters that needing tending. "Do you have any idea where he is now?"

"Nope, and I don't care." She blew a raspberry with her mouth. "I'm slipping into this time-space continuum for a night. Tomorrow we can talk about it. They're playing my song, c'mon dance with me."

Before Jason could answer, Kaitlyn had him out on the dance floor, showing him hip moves that had his heart racing, which had nothing to do with the fast rhythm of the music. It was so out of character for the girl he knew. He wondered if he had stepped into her continuum.

Three blood-pumping dances, one more wine, and much laughter later, Kaitlyn was resting her head on Jason's shoulder, rocking gently to the rhythm of a slow song. She looked up, and immediately their eyes locked. They were oblivious to their surroundings. It was like they were the only ones on the dance floor. Kaitlyn ran her tongue over her bottom lip, inviting him in.

Accepting the invitation, Jason crushed his lips on hers and pulled her tight against him, and she let out a quiet moan. At that moment, time stopped, and nothing else mattered. He'd never wanted anything more in his life. This feeling went far beyond physical. It was much more profound, and it scared the hell out of him. He couldn't take a chance of losing someone he cared for, not again. He still hadn't healed his heart from the loss of his father. Stabbed with sharp realization, Jason pulled away. "I can't," he said and walked back to the table.

Kaitlyn felt sick to her stomach. One moment she was lost in his kiss, and the next, she's on the dance floor left alone, the song still holding lovers close. How embarrassing, not to mention he had hurt her. As she turned around to go back to the table, a nice-looking young man approached her. "Would you like to finish this dance with me?" he asked. Kaitlyn smiled sweetly and, hiding the pain, she took his hand. "I'd love to." Of course, she had no intention of connecting with this man. But since he'd asked and she was angry at Jason, Kaitlyn accepted his offer to dance and made sure she put on a show for the jerk at the top of her list.

Jason sneered when he saw Kaitlyn move into another man's arms. It seemed to him, by the way that Kaitlyn was moving, that she was enjoying his company. A little too much by Jason's observation. It was evident by the monster of jealously rearing its sleazy redhead that this was not ok with him. He wanted to interrupt their interlude, show the guy to the door, and claim her. But he didn't want to cause a scene. And besides, it was his fault. He'd been the idiot who'd left the vulnerable intoxicated girl out on the dance floor.

Just for spite and because she liked the smell of the strange man, Kaitlyn chose to dance with him again. It was better than facing Jason. It was bad enough she'd have to ride back to Cliff and Serena's with him. It was not going to be a fun ride for sure. Why did he have to spoil her happy evening? What did he mean; 'I can't.' Can't finish the dance? She held back her tears, as she wasn't going to let him see her cry.

Kaitlyn returned to the table, offered a cherished smile to her friends, and sent Jason an if-looks-could-kill stare. "Hey, you guys about ready to go?"

"You read my mind. Ever since we've become parents, this mom has changed her night owl wings into yellow morning sparrows. I guess I've gotten used to it," Serena said with a laugh as she grabbed her coat and purse. "You guys follow us."

"Here!" Kaitlyn said abruptly as she practically rammed Jason with her keys. "You can drive."

Jason was still fuming at the image of her in another man's arms stuck in his head. He opened his clenched fist, accepted the keys, and stomped off in a huff, muttering under his breath.

Kaitlyn climbed into the car and slammed the door. Jason, not wanting to be outdone, did the same. The tension was so thick in the car you could cut it with a knife. The tangled emotions wrapped tight, almost strangling the passengers with their anger.

Jason took a deep breath before he started the car, hoping it would diffuse the raging jealous hormones that were taking over. After he had a grip and his hands were steady, Jason inserted the key and turned on the ignition, only to be taunted by a hollow clicking sound. After attempting it two more times, he sat back and shook his head with desperation. "Tatiana, I'm in no mood for games or your tempered attitude."

"What do you think is wrong?" Kaitlyn asked, trying to be civil.

"I don't know. Maybe the classy girl met some fired-up hot rod while we were gone," Jason answered with a condescending tone.

"Well, if she hadn't been left alone, then that might never have happened," Kaitlyn replied spitefully, refusing to look his way.

Their heated discussion was quickly interrupted by another musical message. The song lyrics "*How Can They be so in Love and Still Never See,*" blared out of the radio. "I told you not now," Jason stressed while he turned off the radio.

A loud knock on the passenger window startled Kaitlyn, causing her to jump in her seat. After she realized it was Serena trying to get her attention, Kaitlyn smiled and rolled down the window.

"Everything ok in here?" Serena asked, searching their faces.

"Just dandy," Kaitlyn replied with a spark of sarcasm. "The crazy car won't start and is sending more musical, nonsense messages."

"Hmmm... I see. It's only an observation. But here are my thoughts on what is going on inside. I sense that you both are a bit agitated tonight, for some reason, and that's none of my business. However, letting your frustration ooze out into this car may have caused the already troubled spirit more anguish. The vibes I received earlier told me she was suffering. She needs you as her friends, on her side, not her enemies. Can't you put your differences aside and deal with this later. Hasn't this young spirit been through enough?"

Serena's words hit Kaitlyn in her gut. Everything she had said was right. How had she been so stupid and uncaring to both Jason and Tatiana? What had possessed her to dance with that strange man? That wasn't like her. "She's right," Kaitlyn admitted and looked kindly at Jason.

He, too, felt like a heel. What had drove him to be such a jerk? That was so out of character for him. Something had seized inside him when he'd seen Kaitlyn with another man, and he'd lost control. "Yeah, I guess she is. Hey, listen, I'm sorry, I don't know what came over me."

"I'm sorry too," Kaitlyn admitted, no longer mad at Jason.

"Well, I'll leave you two to work everything out. I have a feeling Tatiana won't be giving you any more trouble tonight." Serena gave a wink and left.

"How do you think she knows that?" Jason asked with a baffled look. Then when he inserted the key, and the car started, his gaze intensified.

Kaitlyn shrugged her shoulders. "She just does."

They both froze when the earlier song lyrics repeated, *"How Can They be so in Love and Still Never See."* Kaitlyn wondered if the musical message was meant for them and not connected to his dad. Had Tatiana been trying to tell them something so obvious? Before she could bring up the subject to Jason, their motorcycle stalker jetted past them. All the lights, and everything that could and did make noise in the car, sounded off. The couple was no longer concerned about the night's event. Their concentration locked in on their speeding predator.

10) TATIANA OPENS UP

"You think we should follow him?" Kaitlyn asked, her eyes squinted to keep an eye on the fading taillight.

"Nah," Jason said, "more than likely, he'll find a side alley. I'm sure he'll appear tomorrow. Besides, I don't know about you, but I'm feeling drained."

"Yeah, let's call it a night," Kaitlyn agreed. Her hand covered her mouth as she yawned.

When they arrived at their friend's house, Serena was waiting in the living room. "I'm not the kind to sugar coat things, as you well know, Katie. So here it is straight. I wasn't sure of your sleeping arrangements, and there's no need to tell me," she expressed, holding up her hand. "There are two spare rooms at the end of the hall upstairs," she noted, pointing to the hand-crafted staircase. "You two can decide. I'm going to bed. There are no kids, so if my maternal clock works on pause mode, I intend on sleeping in until seven." She giggled at her comment. "Good night," the quirky redhead added and left the room, hiding a devious smile as she wondered where her guests would sleep tonight.

Kaitlyn avoided eye contact with Jason and instead reached down and petted her furry companion. Why couldn't Serena have designated their rooms? It would've been so much simpler. Kaitlyn wouldn't be surprised if Serena planned it all out. They were going to have words for sure in the morning. The decision made Kaitlyn uncomfortable. Her intelligent and sensible self, voted for separate rooms. However, her curious and adventurous side was leaning heavily on joining him. Practical self said, 'You just met.' The other half said, 'Just go for it.' Random thoughts sloshed around in the alcohol still present in her head. She finally decided that being under the influence wasn't the best time to react on impulse.

Jason could sense Kaitlyn was battling with the decision. It wasn't easy for him either. Given a choice, he would choose to share her bed. 'What fool wouldn't,' his conscience informed him. Only the fear and uncertainty in her eyes told him she was unsure. Hell, he wasn't sure himself. He raked his fingers through his wavy hair, lost in thought, and seeking guidance from the universe. Minutes later, and still undecided, he held out his hand and broke the awkward silence. "C'mon, let's go to bed."

Kaitlyn took hold, and like a puppet on a string, climbed the stairs with Jason. Both were lost in thought until they came to a stop at the end of the hall between the doors.

The following day Kaitlyn awoke and blinked her eyes. Trying to pull them into focus, she looked at the clock on the nightstand, illuminating the time in a bold color. "It's only 6:30?" Kaitlyn voiced quietly to Gina, who was resting on the end of the bed and in no hurry to get up. She turned and reached her arm to the opposite side of the bed as her foggy head recalled the evening and wondered if she'd make a big mistake. Caught at the crossroads, the wall between the two-bedroom doors had held the fate for the couple. Kaitlyn could tell by the wanting kisses; there was no doubt that he'd made his decision. She had to admit his warm body felt so right against hers. There shouldn't have been any doubt in her mind, but there was. With every moment they stayed locked in the sensual embrace, a brick was lifted from the wall of fear guarding her until almost none remained, and she felt the release of surrender. Driven by passion but still riding on the wave of uncertainty, Kaitlyn pulled away and stared up at Jason. Then with a slight shrug of her shoulder and softness in her eyes, she chose the door closest to her and walked into the room, Gina right on her heels.

She'd been certain her decision had been the right one. But lying here now, Kaitlyn wished his warm body were cuddling hers. She let out a deep sigh at the sight of the disappointment piercing his eyes, which was still etched in her memory. Finally, deciding it wasn't viable to hide in her room all day, Kaitlyn pried herself from the safety of the comfy sleigh bed and started her day. She smiled at the sight of two aspirin on the dresser. "Just like college days," she commented out loud as she read the note. 'Morning, sleepyhead, thought you might need these. You remember our sure-fire remedy for the party-too-harder. I'm supplying the pain meds; the toast and coffee are waiting for you in the kitchen. See you in a few.' Kaitlyn laughed, threw on a light-weight jogging suit, and headed to the kitchen.

The scent of freshly brewed coffee led Kaitlyn to a spacious chef's paradise. Serena had mentioned they both liked to cook, so it was essential to have it equipped with all the latest gadgets and appliances. The chrome stove and matching fridge were the centerpieces for the room. Everything else, including the marble-top island, fell into place. She found Serena at a quaint little corner breakfast nook.

"Good Morning," Serena greeted with a wide grin.

Kaitlyn rolled her eyes at her cheery friend and retrieved a cup from the cupboard. "I'll take the morning, but it's still too early to determine the 'good' part. Still have your daddy's kick-your-butt coffee?"

"You know it! It's the only thing we serve here. I see you chose door number two last night," Serena commented, hiding her smile with the rim of her coffee cup.

"Yeah, about that. Why didn't you just designate rooms?"

Serena chuckled. "What would be the fun in that?"

Kaitlyn rolled her eyes. "Well, it wasn't".

"I don't understand. You had the perfect opportunity and you let it slip through your hands," Serena commented before taking a sip from her cup.

"I'm not ready yet," Kaitlyn quickly answered as she took a seat across from her friend. Then she took a bite of her toast, prepared by Serena. Stuffing her mouth, hoping it would be a sure-fire way to avoid further discussion of that topic. Only she should've known that would never stop her friend.

"When do you think you will be ready?"

Kaitlyn shrugged. "I don't know, but if or when the time does come, I'd like not to be two sheets to the wind. So, are you still planning on taking Tatiana out for a drive?"

"OK, I get that; point taken. And yes, that's the plan. Maybe if I can connect with her terrified spirit, she may open up."

"Good luck with that," Kaitlyn said as she threw her head back with a laugh.

"We'll see. How late are you two in town?"

Kaitlyn glanced at the child's train clock above her head. It was still too early. She focused on the tiny hands; cobwebs and fog still occupied her brain, making it hard to see. "Hmm... probably no later than two. We have to work in the morning."

"I wish you could stay longer," Serena said as she refilled her cup. "Mom's dropping the kids off around 4:00."

"Ahh...bummer. Give them a hug from their aunt Katie. I'll make a point to see them next time."

"Sure thing. Well, I'm going to get a shower and prepare for my drive. There's quiche in the fridge. You can heat a slice in the Micro. The guys already ate. Oh, by the way, Jason said to tell you good morning. Cliff finagled him into tagging along with him on a job bid. Poor Jason." Serena laughed at her last comment. "I need to get this butt in gear." She kissed her friend on the cheek. "Katie dear, get used to it. Love is always messy."

She wasn't in Love. No, that couldn't be, or was it possible? She chewed over the thought, poured another coffee, and sat in the quiet room as she checked in with her emotions.

Jason sat in the cab of Cliff's truck; the stereo speakers rocked the vehicle with a classic rock station while he waited for his friend. Since he was a plumber and familiar with doing business with new clients, Jason knew that these discussions could be time eaters, especially when working with a meticulous man who wanted to go through every detail. From what Jason understood, Cliff's customer was the owner of a tool store looking to expand.

Jason didn't mind waiting. It gave him time to check his emails and social media pages. Only he was having a difficult time keeping his mind focused. Right now, it was back at the house with some beautiful short-haired redhead. He had wanted her to join him last night, but the fear in her eyes led him to believe that she didn't feel the same. He could still hear the creaky door closing, leaving him alone and confused in the hallway, shut out of her night. He hoped it wasn't out of her life too.

All the signs were there. Kaitlyn had been in his arms, bodies pressed together, and with every kiss and every sigh, he was positive she'd choose him. He'd like to think that something other than him was holding her back. Maybe a past relationship was to blame for the protective walls she'd built around her heart. They'd never talked about it, but perhaps it was time he brought it up. He was still a little apprehensive about starting a relationship himself because part of his heart was still grieving over his dad. However, he was fairly certain, the other part was beginning to fall. Something shifted last night when he had seen Kaitlyn in another man's arms. Maybe his mom was right. It was time to move on and let the pent-up anger go, it wasn't healthy. It kept him stuck and stagnant. He decided he was going to ride out this mystery and see where it all ended. He'd come this far down the backcountry roads, but was he ready for a relationship with some dangerous curves?

Kaitlyn was outside tossing the ball for the dogs when Serena pulled up in Tatiana. She threw the ball one last time and watched as Gina and Brody raced to get it. Even though the yellow lab had a few years on Gina, he could keep up and sometimes even beat her to the ball.
"Well, how did she do?" Kaitlyn apprehensively asked as she patted the car's hood.

Serena smiled as she removed the bonnet holding back her wild red curls. "Not bad after she learned who the boss was. The little rebel tried to take me through a car wash, a fast-food restaurant, and a football field. She has determination; I'll give her that."

"Oh, no!" Kaitlyn replied, covering her mouth to hide a grin. "I warned you she is stubborn."

"She tested my limits just like any teenager would do, but soon found out I wasn't going to give in," Serena said. "After we got that settled, she released the tight hold on the emergency brake and let me in." Serena stepped outside the car, shook out her hair, and stretched her legs. Her eyes then turned sad. "Her spirit is surrounded by darkness. Not exactly evil, more of where she exists in this realm. Now, this is only a theory, as I'm new to reading car spirits, but I surmise this little girl's body could be or was either buried or locked away somewhere like a trunk or closet."

Kaitlyn shivered, wrapped her arms around herself, and rubbed the goosebumps caused by the eerie possibility. "Oh, poor girl, and I've been so mean to her."

Serena patted her friend's shoulder. "Katie dear, you didn't know, and I'm sure Tatiana isn't holding it against you."

"I also got a glimpse of a nice-looking man; I speculate in his late forties. It was extraordinary, like nothing I've ever experienced before."

"What do you mean?" Kaitlyn asked, her curiosity pulling her closer.

Serena closed her eyes and raised her head as she described the image. "What strikes me as odd is that this man didn't have a certain glow like all the other spirits I've connected with. He was sitting at a table, his eyes empty and staring into space."

Kaitlyn's eyes lit up. "You think it could be Jason's dad? Is he alive?"

Serena opened her eyes. "I don't know the answer to either question. I've never tried to reach a spirit inside a car. And on top of that, this girl's spirit is sending me images. It could be that because I am seeing them through another spirit, the images were distorted. Let me say that I wouldn't give up hope, but you might not blast this news to Jason, at least not yet."

"Probably a good idea," Kaitlyn said, her excitement tamed by Serena's comment. "Was that all you found out?"

"No, there's one more thing," Serena commented as she bent down to retrieve the ball from Brody. "You know how Tatiana likes to send clues through song lyrics?"

"Yes."

"There were three different songs that popped in. All had to do with the word 'sharp.' This is just my hunch, but I think it might be a street name or a person's name. You told me that she'd already referenced it in two other songs, so it must be important." Serena tossed the ball and laughed as both dogs raced to retrieve it.

Kaitlyn shook her head. "With all that I know now, I still haven't moved ahead in this mess. These are just scattered pieces to a puzzle that doesn't even have the outline framed. How am I supposed to find what piece fits where? They might as well all be corner pieces," she voiced in frustration.

"Katie, I'm sure it will all come together somehow. Talk to Jason, maybe he has some ideas. Lay out everything you've learned, from start to finish. Once you have the four corner pieces, the rest should fall into place," she expressed with a wink. "I hope that helps," Serena said as she handed Kaitlyn the keys, then smiled wide when she spotted Cliff's truck pull up the drive. "Hey babe," she said, greeting him with a kiss as he stepped out of the cab.

Kaitlyn noticed Jason and wanted to bolt like a lightning flash to his side, but instead stayed strong, forced a smile, and prepared for the storm.

"Hey," Jason said, slipping his hands in his pockets as he walked over to where Kaitlyn was standing.

"Hi," Kaitlyn responded, her mind at a loss. Instead of engaging, she turned her attention to Cliff and Serena.

"I took the lady for a drive," Serena said, breaking up the awkward silence.

"Yeah, how'd she do?" Jason asked.

"OK, when she realized I wasn't a pushover." Serena's laughter lightened the mood. "I'll let Katie fill you in on your drive back." She took hold of Cliff's hand and said, "Come up to the house. I'll make us all lunch while you get packed. I know you two want to get on the road soon."

"Sounds good," Kaitlyn replied, walking a few feet in front of Jason, keeping her attention on the happy couple.

After lunch, Kaitlyn and Jason gathered their belongings, loaded the car, and said their goodbyes. Ten miles out of town, the humming vehicle was the only sound that filled the front seat. All was still until the car veered off to the shoulder and stopped.

"Why are we stopping here? Is there something wrong with the car?" Kaitlyn asked with a frown, glancing around the vehicle, and then to Jason for answers.

"I don't know, why don't you ask your girlfriend," Jason replied, attempting to start the engine.

"Isn't there something you can do to make her move? We can't sit here alongside the road."

"Well, I'm not going to get out and push her, but you can be my guest," he answered smugly.

"Ha ha. Why do you think Tat is doing this?" Kaitlyn asked, laying her head in her hands, ignoring all of Jason's sarcastic comments.

Jason turned his head towards her. "I don't know; maybe she's concerned and wants us to work things out."

"I'm getting tired of being controlled by a vehicle. Can't you threaten her or use your boyish charm?" Kaitlyn pleaded.

"I don't think that will work this time. She seems adamant about holding her ground." He could see that this stubborn move of Tatiana's was irritating Kaitlyn. However, he was happy to have the opportunity to talk to Kaitlyn, and this way, she couldn't make excuses and run. He also felt that the car was aware of this and was helping him.

"Argh..." she expressed sincerely.

"Why don't we give her what she wants. Let's talk about last night, about us."

Kaitlyn swallowed hard. "I didn't know there was an us. Is there supposed to be an us?"

"That's what we need to find out." Jason moved closer to Kaitlyn. "I like you, and I'm fairly sure you like me too. At least that what your kisses were saying last night, and kisses never lie." He brushed a strand of hair away from her eyes.

Kaitlyn shivered under his touch. "Damn lips," she said with a nervous giggle, "don't know when to mind their own business. Yes, I like you, Jason, but a relationship right now would be messy and complicated."

"How would you know? Do you have some clairvoyant talent I don't know about?"

"Nooooo. I'm just not ready for serious. It takes a lot of work, time, and dedication. And then when you give your all...," she said, looking away, after revealing too much.

Jason cupped her chin with his hands and turned her toward him. He could sense she was trying to shut him out and avoid getting any deeper. "What happened when you gave your all? Why don't you tell me about him?"

"About him?" Kaitlyn replied with a high pitch.

"Yeah, the man that caused you to build a shelter around your heart."

"You don't want to hear about my relationship drama, and besides it's over and done. I've moved on." Liar, Liar repeated in her head.

"Yes, I'm interested. I want to know the ghost I'm up against. And are you sure you've moved on?"

She didn't like talking about her personal life and had only shared her story with a select few. "It's really nothing. If you think it will get Tat to move, then I will tell you." As she was formulating the words in her mind, a flash in her side mirror caused her to pause. "I think motorcycle-man is trying to catch up with us. He must've got a late start today." She turned to Jason. "He is going to be so pissed to see us sitting alongside the road, and have to pass by." Kaitlyn chuckled at the image.

Jason checked out the trail in the rearview mirror.

"Where's that pen you had earlier? Let's get his license plate number. I have a friend at the DMV that owes me a favor."

"There should be one in the side pocket of the door. I have some paper inside the console."

"What's this?" Kaitlyn asked, taking the pen and business card he handed her.

Jason shrugged and said, "It was hooked to the pen when I pulled it out. You can write the number on the back."

"I've got an idea," Kaitlyn cheered. "Let's smile and wave at him when he passes." Then she turned the card over.

The motorcycle zipped past them, and to their surprise, he waved back. "I got the number," Kaitlyn said. Killed by curiosity, she turned the card over and read it out loud. "Steven Simon Harpe, JR. Certified and licensed roofer. Your around the corner, neighbor. We go above and beyond to keep your family covered and safe."

"Where did that come from?" Jason asked.

"I don't know," Kaitlyn replied as she searched her mind's database. "It must've been the one Simon gave to me the day he practically climbed into the car at the coffee shop. Guess it fell into the pocket of the door."

Jason sat back in the seat; his body tensed at the thought of the jerk. "Well, we can't do anything about finding him now, so how about filling me in on what happened in your last relationship?" Jason said, placing his attention back on Kaitlyn, who was still studying the card.

But another distraction, an ah-ha moment, caused Kaitlyn to divert her attention away from the painful memory. "I think I have it!" Kaitlyn screamed out, her eyes wide as saucers as she stared at Jason. "I know the meaning of the word 'sharp.'" Serena's words echoed in her mind. 'Find the four corners, and the rest will fall into place.' Had she just found one or more of them? She shivered at the thought. Did Serena know more than what she'd revealed?

11) THE DISCOVERY

"That's odd. I wonder why she started back up?" Jason asked, trying to take control of the car as it merged onto the highway. He had hoped to have a few more minutes with Kaitlyn.

Kaitlyn shrugged. "Maybe she recognized the name on the card."

"What name on the card?"

"It's really simple, and it's been there all the time," Kaitlyn said excitedly. "The name written on this card is Steven Simon Harpe, JR. If you take the S in the first or middle name and place it in front of the last name, you get Sharpe."

Jason shot a glance at Kaitlyn. "Great work! That's what Tatiana has been trying to get across to us all this time? One thing bothers me, though."

"What's that?"

"Simon seems so young. How do you think he's tied to Tatiana?" Jason asked, tossing the thought around in his head.

Kaitlyn sat back in her seat and stretched the seatbelt, securing her in. "I'm not sure, and Tat hasn't given us much to go on. Unless...," she pondered a passing thought, switching gears into serious detective mode. "He's a scout, keeping an eye on us and reporting back to someone." She drummed her manicured fingers on the console. "The questions are who and why?"

"I may have a possible answer for the why," Jason interjected. "What if there is something in this car?"

"I like your way of thinking. But what?" Kaitlyn asked, racking her brain excitedly as the thrill of getting closer drew her in. She perused the car, already searching.

Jason let out a heavy sigh as his mind also searched for answers. He startled Kaitlyn when his hand purposely hit the steering wheel. "Weren't there a couple of song lyrics that are still hanging? Like the fire ring?"

Kaitlyn giggled. "You mean Ring of Fire?"

"Yes, that's it. Let's just say that whoever it is lost a ring or a circular object in this car."

"Or maybe it's Tatiana's and has their fingerprints on it," Kaitlyn added. "You know we're good." She commented, throwing him a high five in the air.

Jason listened as the car filled with Kaitlyn's musical laughter.

The more he was with her, the more he longed for her. She was so natural, funny, smart, and so sexy. What he marveled at the most was that she didn't even realize it. Funny how life works. He'd never pictured himself with someone like her, but now he couldn't imagine his life without her. He had to break through her walls.

"We are good, good together," Jason admitted, sending a caring smile her way. "So, are you going to tell me about the guy that broke your heart?"

Kaitlyn froze and stared out the window. She'd thought that vehicle had already passed by and was miles away. Wanting to avoid the heartache, she asked, "What about the Ring?"

"There isn't much more to discuss. When we get back, we can search the car. But for now, I'd like you to tell me about him."

It was obvious he wasn't going to drop it. "You are so persistent. But if I must, I must." Kaitlyn said, shaking her head. She knew he wasn't going to stop pestering her, so she pulled on her inner strength, kept her eyes straight ahead, and stepped into the past. "We met about six years ago in college. I fell fast and hard; he was the one for me. At least, that's what my heart led me to believe. We were inseparable. Every moment apart, I longed for the next time we'd be together. Our friends deemed us the perfect couple. We hardly ever fought, and when we did, it was quick and short-lived." Kaitlyn paused, took a swig from her water bottle, and then continued.

"Everything was going well until he was offered a job out of state. Backup a minute," she said, rolling her left index finger over her right. "He had majored in engineering and, after he'd graduated, found a job at a small firm. Ok, back on track. His work ethic and quality of work earned him a position at the corporate office in LA. He was sure our relationship could withstand the long-distance struggles. However, I was apprehensive, and even though it would break my heart, I thought about a temporary separation. He had faith that we could make it work, and I, like a lovesick puppy, agreed to give it a try."

"I take it the relationship didn't do so well," Jason commented.

Kaitlyn, suddenly more relaxed and relieved all at the same time, turned to Jason. "Well, we stayed in regular contact at first, but as time went on, the talks got shorter, personal visits became fewer. After six months, we were barely communicating. But it wasn't because I didn't try." Kaitlyn turned away; she knew this next part was going to be the hardest. "Out of the blue, I decided to call him. It had been a while since we'd talked, and I missed him. I'll tell you my heart certainly wasn't prepared for the shock on the other end of the line."

"What happened?" Jason asked, now immersed in the story.

"A female answered his phone. She said hello in a sexy voice, noted it wasn't her phone, and asked if I wanted to leave a message for her fiancé, Bryan. I hung up immediately. Tears of loss flowed down my cheeks. Then and there, I knew we were over. Probably had been for a while, only my heart hadn't been informed of the news."

Jason reached out his hand, found Kaitlyn's, and gave it a gentle squeeze.

"I'm sorry, what a jerk. Not much of a man to string you along and leave you in limbo."

Kaitlyn shrugged. "It wasn't meant to be," she said, trying to make light of the memory. "Thank you for listening. It wasn't easy to talk about something so personal, but I'm glad I did."

 "I'm happy you told me, and you never have to worry. I'd never do that to you. My mommy raised me better than that." He gave her hand another squeeze and let go.

Kaitlyn didn't know how to respond. She could feel her heart ready to fall, but there was still some fear nestled inside her. The words were there. Everything she needed and wanted presented itself in a handsome and caring package, only a couple of feet away. All she had to do was reach out. But her mind quickly changed gears at Jason's next comment.

"Well, would you look over there," he said, pointing up ahead at the motorcycle stopped on the shoulder. "Seems like our friend blew a tire," he said with a smug expression.

"Ahh... poor guy," she replied sarcastically.

They stared and smiled at the frustrated rider, standing next to his stock Harley in distress. A not-so-friendly finger returned their friendly wave.

After they celebrated their awarded moment, Kaitlyn decided it was time for Jason to spill some of his own beans. She turned toward him, put her foot under her behind, and prepared herself. "Well, since I've given you a blast from my past, I think it's fair you do the same thing. I'm talking about relationship history, marriages, hook-ups, illegitimate kids."

Jason smirked. "Not much to tell. I've led a simple, mostly drama-free life. I've had girlfriends, and only one became serious. We came close to getting married, but she dumped me when she found out I didn't fit into her mold. And I don't believe there are any adorable little humans roaming the earth with my eyes."

"What about your nose?" she teased, playfully running her finger down his nose.

He sighed, took her hand, kissed it, and linked his with hers. "So, do I pass? What do you say? You in?"

"Let's just say I'm dipping my foot in the pool." Kaitlyn fell back in her seat.

"I'll take it," Jason replied happily.

Kaitlyn smiled, beaming with happiness and joy.

She could feel the rope of fear and uncertainty slip from her grip. Not to say strings of apprehension weren't still hanging on, but she could live with the loose ends. What relationship didn't have them. Oh my, she thought, I'm in a relationship. Fear started to creep back, but she pushed it away. It wasn't going to rule her life anymore.

Kaitlyn was pulled from her thoughts when a song of celebration rang through the speakers.

"I think we made Tat's day," Jason commented, patting the dashboard. "You never told me what Serena found out on her drive."

Kaitlyn gave him a sideways glance. "Well, I was a little occupied with other topics." She chuckled and then told him about Serena's experience, but left out the part about his dad.

"Crazy. If Serena is right on any account, Tatiana has suffered a lot of pain," he expressed with anger. "When I first started this journey, it was with the hope of finding my father, but now I want to find the guy that hurt this little girl and bring him to justice."

"Me too! How do you suppose we do that?"

"I'm not sure, but maybe after I pay Simon a visit, I'll have the answer or a plan in mind."

Kaitlyn patted his leg, "Please promise me you'll be careful. We don't know what we're up against here." The fury she saw blazing in his eyes alarmed her.

At that moment, Kaitlyn realized Serena had been right. She did love him, and now another fear was waiting in line. The thought of losing him scared her more than ever.

"I'll be careful, don't worry," he assured her. Jason rolled down the window and leaned his arm out the window. The cold air felt good. He had let some of his anger go and knew it had frightened Kaitlyn. He needed to work on getting that in check.

The rest of the ride home, when the car wasn't filled with get-to-know-you chatter, favorite tunes were rocking the vehicle. For the time being, all three were in a contented state as Tatiana guided them back home.

When Jason pulled down Kaitlyn's road, he felt a little down.

He didn't want this time with her to end, but he needed to get back to the farm. Ever since his dad had disappeared, he'd taken up the slack. Maybe he'd let his mom hire some help. She'd suggested it, but he'd been so pigheaded at the time.

It was just too much for them to handle. This road trip had been a blessing in disguise; not only had he found his love, but he was ready to work on letting go of his dad and deciding to move on with his life.

When the car stopped, Jason turned to Kaitlyn and took her hands in his. "Thank you."

"For what?" she asked with bewilderment.

"In two days, you have shown me how to love again and let go and move on. Key elements I was striving for the last two years, but I was stuck and didn't see any way out."

"Wow! I didn't know I possessed so much power," she teased.

"I'm serious." Before Kaitlyn could respond, he leaned in and kissed her ready-to-talk lips.

After they unloaded the car, Kaitlyn walked Jason to his car. She wrapped her hands around him, slipped her hands into his back pockets, and gazed into his loving eyes. "If we are confessing, you also helped me overcome some fears this weekend, too, like facing my past and tearing down walls.

Not bad for a handsome annoyance," she teased, then met his lips and gave him a sendoff kiss, one she'd bet he couldn't forget.

The next day, Kaitlyn fell back into her regular work pattern. She had been warned last week that it was going to start getting busy. That was an understatement, as a line of customers, ten people long, if they weren't glued to their phones, greeted her at the door. She barely had time to unlock the door before the first one stepped up to the counter. A classic car show was coming into town in a couple of weeks. Everyone with show-quality cars needed parts ordered and vehicle inspection appointments. The stream of customers kept her running and hopping, and by the end of the day, she was exhausted. She had been smart to ask for time off from her accounting job. Juggling two jobs now would be more than she could handle.

The madhouse at work caused a break in her newfound relationship.

Even Jason was putting in overtime by helping where and when he could, leaving them no time together, except for a stolen kiss or hidden touch during a spare unguarded moment.

When Friday came, Kaitlyn took a deep breath as she locked the doors at 7:00. Another long day. This week had just about done her in, and it looked like she was going to repeat it next week. She would've loved to spend the evening with Jason and Gina by her side. However, her mom had been hinting about a Friday family dinner all week. Kaitlyn felt obligated, mainly since she'd hadn't spent much time with them lately. She knew her mom was expecting Jason, but he was donating any open hours he had with his mom. So, as much as she'd like a cold beer and pizza kind of night, snuggled up to her guy, she'd settle for a chaotic but always entertaining evening with her family.

Jason arrived at Kaitlyn's early Saturday morning. He had taken a chance by surprising her and hoped she'd be up.

He almost dropped the coffee when she greeted him at the door, half asleep and dressed in a skimpy nightshirt.

His heart skipped a beat at the wild red-haired sexy mess with a come-get-me-smile. "You are so beautiful, and the best part is you're mine." He set the coffees on a nearby end-table, pulled her into his arms, and kissed her with a raw and primal need.

Kaitlyn hadn't expected Jason so early, so she was caught off guard when he appeared at her door. He was looking hot as ever, and she could imagine his thoughts of the chaotic mess answering the door. But her hesitation was melted away with his loving touch and kisses.

Realizing he may have overstepped her boundaries, Jason quieted the kiss and embraced her in a hug. She had just broken through her protective shell, and he didn't want her to get scared and rebuild it. "Here, I brought you coffee, just in case I was too early, and was in for a scolding," he laughed, handing her a paper cup.

Kaitlyn took a sip and said, "Yummy, mocha, my fav. You did well. I'll let you off the hook this time," she teased and invited him in.

"Am I too early?" Jason asked, knowing the answer to the question already, but he wasn't about to leave.

"Saturday's brunch was canceled due to Friday dinner last night, so I was taking the opportunity to sleep in. No worries though, sleep is so overrated sometimes," she said with a dismissive wave. "Thanks for the coffee. Can I offer you some breakfast? I was planning on scrambled eggs and veggies."

"Twist my arm," he said, holding it out.

Kaitlyn laughed at his comment as she moved into the kitchen and started preparing the meal. She loved her place; it offered her a view of the man taking comfort in her home. The sight of him kicked back on the sofa, capturing Gina's heart, filled Kaitlyn's heart with joy.

She wished the car craziness was all over and things were back in place with her life. She felt guilty, holding out information about the chance his father may be alive. Of course, that wasn't a sure thing. She couldn't live with herself if she gave him hope, and it turned out to be false information. It would be like breaking his heart all over again. It was a pain she wouldn't want to instill in anyone. But on the other hand, what if he was alive? Was it fair to keep that information from him?

Kaitlyn had wrangled with this dilemma ever since they'd left Astoria and concluded there was no right or wrong answer. She just hoped he'd never find out that she knew.

After they ate, she and Jason spent most of the afternoon searching the inside of Tatiana for a circular item or anything that might be a clue. They looked in every hidden corner and the smallest spaces and all they had to show for their wasted time was a few candy wrappers and an old matchbook.

"I don't understand," Jason said, scratching his head. "I was sure we'd find something. Maybe that song had nothing to do with finding my dad."

Kaitlyn placed her hand on Jason's shoulder. "I don't believe she'd send us a useless clue."

Jason shrugged. "Then what does it mean? I've racked my brain, and nothing is coming to mind."

"I don't know. I feel your frustration," Kaitlyn answered as her eyes locked on the matchbook. "Did your dad smoke?" she asked while reaching for the old package.

"Occasionally he'd light up a pipe, but he always used a lighter that belonged to my grandfather. He never did it around mom. She hated the smell," Jason added, recalling the memory.

 Kaitlyn flipped the cover back. "There is a phone number and the initials SS," she said, showing Jason. "It must be important, or was at one time, because someone drew a circle around them."

"Hmm... maybe the initials SS represent Steven Sharpe, and the phone number could be his from back then. That could be a big stretch, but it's something to go on."

Kaitlyn gave Jason a serious look as she shook her head. "I don't think you're reaching too far; in fact, you might be closer than you think."

"Matches make fire, and there is a circle around the initials and number. Let's get the final vote. Hey, Tatiana, am I right?" The flashing lights on the dash and flipping wipers settled the debate.

"You think this guy, Steven or Simon, whatever his name is, has been following us to get his hands on these old things?" Jason asked, rolling the package in his fingers.

"Could be he's scared of being caught," Kaitlyn surmised, putting the clues together. "With the modern technology available today, they can trace his prints and match his DNA. His prints could be all over this matchbook."

Jason raised his brows. "Can this tiny little item do all that?"

"Yes, and I hope our prints haven't destroyed the evidence," she said with gritted teeth. "Let's call the number." With that said, Kaitlyn retrieved her phone from her purse and keyed in the number. Then they both waited anxiously for someone to answer. After five rings, a friendly female voice greeted them. "Stretch and Sleek Auto Detailing, how can I help you?"

"Oh, sorry, I must've called the wrong number," Kaitlyn replied and ended the call. "Bummer," she sighed.

"Shoot," Jason agreed. "That's where dad took his cars. I don't believe there's any connection." He dropped his head and looked at his feet. "It looked so promising. We are no further ahead."

Before Kaitlyn could comment, her cell phone buzzed. "It's Serena," she said, greeting her friend.

 "Hey, girlfriend, what's up?"

"I was checking to see if you found anything more about the car and the spirit?" Serena replied.

"I'll leave you to your call. Do you want a soda? Jason asked.

Kaitlyn smiled, nodded, and returned to her call.

Kaitlyn shared with Serena what had occurred on their trip back home and their discovery today.

"I just can't stress enough. You can't tell Jason about his dad. Not until we know for sure."

"Don't worry. I haven't said anything to Jason about his dad."

"Good. Well, I'd better go. The kids are fighting over some silly thing. Please keep me in the loop. Love you, girl."

After Kaitlyn said goodbye, she turned and practically ran into Jason. Oh no, she frantically thought, looking into his hollow eyes. He had heard her. She felt like a puppy with her tail between her legs and imagined her flushed forehead was flashing the word 'guilty' in bold print.

12) BRAINSTORM

A few miles down the road from Kaitlyn's, a heated discussion was blazing between father and son.

"Another mission you botched up, boy," the older gentlemen ranted. He picked up the burning cigar from the ashtray. He drew in a long drag and blew the smoke toward the yellowed, stained walls. "I told you to take my pickup. It's more reliable than that piece of junk you call a motorcycle. Next time..."

"There isn't going to be a next time," Simon yelled as his fist hit the table. "I'm tired of being your spy. Do it yourself."

The older gentlemen smiled a toothless grin and threw back a shot of liquid courage. He waited for the numbing to take effect, then lunged across the table and latched on to his son's collar. "You listen to me; you will do what I say, or I will cut you off. You'll never get another cent from me."

Simon pulled away from his father's reach and ripped his shirt in the process. He downed his half-filled beer and sat back, his anger flaring. "You can't do that. The money is mine. Mom left it for me in her will."

"Did your little pea brain forget that she made me the trustee until you turn twenty-five? The way you're going through it, there won't be anything left in the account." Steven took another long drag from his cigar, exhaled, and filled the air. "It's your choice. No shirt off my back," he said, fighting off another coughing attack as he reached for his inhaler on the ash-covered desk. "Now, I have an idea if you're ready to listen."

"Fine!" Simon sharply replied.

"I figured you'd see it my way," Steven commented, a smirk pasted on his face. "Now listen up. You want to take notes?"

"No, I don't need to take any notes," Simon starkly replied.

"Ok, here is the plan." With that, father and son studied the layout diagram for the plan that Steven assured would be foolproof.

13) BROKEN

Kaitlyn stood in shock. Oh no, she was busted. How had she let this happen? Serena was going to kill her. That was if there was anything left of her. The look on Jason's face already had her in pieces. Even though she was sure he'd heard her, playing dumb was her strongest defense right now. It was a slim chance, but maybe she'd misread him. A girl could always hope, she thought.

"Oh, Jason, you startled me. Thanks for the soda. I'm parched, and I have this tickle in my throat," Kaitlyn said, faking a cheerful voice. Then she popped the top and let the cold liquid quench her dry throat.

"What did Serena want?" Jason asked inquisitively.

"Oh, you know, just wanted to catch up. She was able to grab a few minutes away from her kids for some girl talk. I don't want to bore you with unnecessary details. So, where were we?" Kaitlyn asked, hoping to push the topic aside.

Jason slipped his hands into his pockets and gave a sideways grin. "That's ok, bore me with the details, especially if they concern my dad. So, what is it you're not supposed to tell me about him?"

Kaitlyn froze. Yikes, he had heard her. Standing at the crossroads of telling or not telling him, she released her stoic state and replied.

"Jason, could you trust me here? Please don't insist I tell you now," she pleaded.

"If it concerns my dad, good or bad, I want to know."

Kaitlyn patted the sofa inviting Jason to sit next to her, then let out a long breath. "Serena saw someone in her mind's eye that she thought might have been your dad. However, it was hard for her to tell for sure because she saw it through Tatiana's spirit. It's rare for that to happen, and it was the first time she's experienced anything like it."

"I don't understand what that means?" Jason asked with a baffled look.

"I don't get it either. Serena said it didn't have the same color aura as a regular spirit, so she mentioned he might not be in spirit form."

Jason quickly rose from the couch, his eyes wide with wonder. "Are you saying that my dad might be alive?"

Kaitlyn shrugged, "She didn't know. That's why I didn't say anything."

Jason moved away from Kaitlyn and shot her a look of disappointment. "Why, Kaitlyn, wouldn't you tell me?" he asked loudly, his arms raised high in the air. "I thought you were my friend; we were partners on the same team."

Kaitlyn lowered her head and avoided the hurt in his eyes. "I didn't want you to get your hopes up."

"That's not your decision to make. Has it occurred to you that I might want the hope, even if it may be false? It's more comfortable to ride on hope than sit in pain and despair and give up. You had no right!" Jason stated, his fists balled at his side.

"Jason," Kaitlyn softly said as she wiped a tear, one of many streaking down her cheek. "I'm sorry, we both felt it was the best thing to do at the time, especially when Serena wasn't certain the spirit, she'd seen was your dad."

"Well, thank you. It's nice to know that you two, who have no idea what I've been going through, can decide for me," Jason replied in a sarcastic tone. "I'm not a little child, Kaitlyn."

"I never said you were," Kaitlyn answered, getting a little irritated with his childlike behavior. "And we were not deciding for you, and I never meant to hurt you."

"Well, you did," Jason answered, glaring at Kaitlyn. "I'd appreciate it, next time, that is, if there is one, that you include me instead of determining my fate. Now, if you'll excuse me, I need to get going, or would you like to have a say in that as well?" He stood still for a moment glaring at Kaitlyn, then stormed out of the house, got into his truck, slammed the door, and drove off, leaving flying rock in his wake.

Kaitlyn watched until she could no longer see his taillights, then grabbed her head. What just happened? How had she been so careless? He'd probably never forgive her or talk to her again, and she couldn't blame him, yet at the same time, in her heart, she felt she'd done the right thing. She was also going to be on Serena's bad list as well. Kaitlyn curled up on the couch, cuddled up with Gina, sobbing as she played the night back in her head.

The blood was pumping through Jason's veins; his head was pounding so hard, like a time bomb ready to explode. He wanted so bad to hit something. How could she have betrayed him like that? He trusted her, and she let him down. He knew it had been a bad idea to let his guard down and invite another woman into his heart. They always meant trouble with a capital T. He'd thought she was different, but that assumption had been wrong.

Jason was not ready to go home and needed someone to talk to or at least vent to, and his uncle was a prime candidate. Ever since his dad has passed, Bill had been there for him.

He parked his car at the garage and took a couple of minutes to sort through his thoughts and reach a calmer level.

When he had his emotions somewhat in check, he went to find his uncle.

Bill had his head under the hood of a shiny red Chevrolet Camaro and pulled it out when he heard Jason's heavy footsteps. "She sure is a beauty, 1967 eight-cylinder, muscle power. They just don't make them like this anymore," he said with a smile as he wiped his hands on an oil-stained rag. "Hey boy, what brings you by this evening? Is everything alright with your mom?"

"Yes, she's fine," Jason quickly replied to his uncle, hoping to wipe away the concern and worry on his face.

"Then what? Never mind, I'm familiar with that look, girl trouble. You want to talk about it?"

Jason paced back and forth in the small aisleway in the garage as he spewed out his anger. "Oooh, she makes me so mad. I thought she was different than all the rest, that I could trust her. But noooo! The nerve of her, she says she knows what I need and want. If I want to get my hopes up, then I darn well have that right."

Bill put his hand out in front of his chest to stop Jason's nervous walk. "Hey boy, slow down; I can't understand your grumbling. What in the world could that sweet girl have done to get you so riled?"

"Huh... sweet... right. That's what Kaitlyn leads you to believe, and then when you least expect it, she gives you a sucker punch," Jason replied, pushing his fist in his stomach. "Anyway, it's a long story. I'm not going into details, but she might have reason to believe my dad is alive and kept the information from me."

"Again," Bill said, his face twisted in misbelief and confusion.

"She knew that my dad may be alive and didn't tell me cause she wanted to spare my feelings if it wasn't true," Jason replied, mocking her statement.

"I'm still confused." Bill stepped up close and gazed into his nephew's eyes. "You been drinking or doing drugs?" Bill asked with concern.

"No, I'm perfectly sober and straight. I don't expect you to understand. Sorry to interrupt your afternoon," Jason said, turning to go.

"Wait," Bill called after seeing his nephew's long face. "I don't know what's going on or understand it, but if it's weighing on your mind, then it must be important. So, take the shackles off, sit down and tell me what's eating at you."

Jason froze and stared at his uncle. Darn, he just wanted to leave, but the softness in this uncle's voice changed his mind, and he took a seat on the bench.

"So, let me get this straight. Kaitlyn knows your dad is alive and didn't tell you. What was her reason?" Bill asked with compassion, humoring the confused and trouble young man.

Jason lowered his head. "She said something about not wanting to get my hopes up. She didn't want me to get hurt."

"Hmm...," Bill mumbled. "I don't see any harm in that. It sounds like she was trying to protect you."

"That's just it, I don't need to be protected," Jason remarked, his temper slowly creeping back.

"I understand," Bill said, offering a comforting pat on his shoulder, then he pondered the situation for a moment. "Are you going to tell your mother about Greg?"

Jason thought a moment. "Probably not right away, wouldn't want to take a chance of breaking her heart again."

Bill shook his head. "Let me get this straight. It's ok for you to withhold information from your mom to protect her, but it's not ok for Kaitlyn. I think some double standards are going on here, boy."

"That's different," Jason answered, pleading his case.

"How so?" Bill answered, his arms folded at his chest.

"It just is," or was it? Jason asked himself. Kaitlyn was only doing what she thought was right. The anger had been so blinding he hadn't been able to see the big picture. He ran his hands through his hair as all the harsh words he'd thrown at Kaitlyn came flying back at him.

Jason turned toward his uncle. "You've given me some things to chew on. Thanks for listening. I should probably go," he said as he hugged his uncle.

Bill patted his nephew on the back. "Anytime my boy. I'm always here for you."

Sunday, Kaitlyn moped around the house and sheltered herself from the outside world. She kept her cell phone on silent and avoided any social media groups, curled up in a ball on the couch, and hugged the pillow tightly for comfort. How was she going to show up at work? Calling in sick wasn't an option; they were too busy at the shop. She wouldn't do that to Bill. A student was helping after school, and he needed training. She could only hope that Jason wouldn't come into the shop. Given his reaction yesterday, he would probably stay far away. "Oh, Gina, what am I going to do?" she asked her trusted friend, lying next to her for support.

The next morning at 7:00, Kaitlyn dressed in her Jeans, work T-shirt and tennis shoes, opened the store. She'd shown up early to beat the crowd and get caught up on paperwork and emails. Everybody needed stuff yesterday. She could give the small tedious tasks to the student worker, which would allow her time to wait on customers.

By 8:00, a line of ten plus people waited outside the door. Kaitlyn turned on the open sign, unlocked the door, and took a deep breath to prepare herself for the tornado about to come flying into the shop. Two hours later, a break in the flow allowed her a few minutes to rest. Her head was buzzing; a headache was brewing on the surface. Lack of sleep was undoubtedly the culprit. Kaitlyn grabbed a snack, hydrated herself with water, and downed a couple of aspirin. She kicked back in a chair and closed her eyes. It had been a hectic morning, but at least it kept her from thinking about Jason.

She'd looked up only a couple of times, hoping to see him walk through the door with his playful grin. But no luck. He hadn't sent a text, called, sent a homing pigeon or smoke signals. He was truly angry with her. Maybe when he cooled off, they could talk. Right now, the office was calling to her.

Jason did all he could to avoid Kaitlyn all afternoon. When he was at the shop, he stayed outside. He had wanted to talk with her many times but wasn't sure how to approach her. He'd been a jerk, not to say she'd been right about her decision, but in a way, he understood why she'd done it. Last night he'd keyed in her number multiple times but couldn't force himself to hit the call button. He played formulate-and-delete text, over and over. He couldn't find the right words to make it better. His tossing and turning late into the early morning had him dragging, and still into the afternoon. He was walking in a fog. He could hardly focus on his plumbing project. His heart just wasn't in it; he'd left it at Kaitlyn's when he'd walked out. He wondered if she'd thought of him at all during the day.

Kaitlyn flew through her day and was relieved when her last customer approached the counter. He needed some parts for his classic car.

They were still attached to the vehicle, so she'd need to take a picture, get some id numbers, and order them tomorrow. She'd agreed to follow him out after locking up.

Kaitlyn put Gina in her car, ignoring her soft growl, and then followed the stranger out to the car. It wasn't the first time her job had required her to do some hands-on work. This week she'd welcomed the break from the counter and enjoyed seeing some great classic cars. She and Jason had planned on going to the event. A deep sigh penetrated the chills down her body as thoughts of him passed through her mind, but she pushed it aside and concentrated on the task at hand.

Kaitlyn walked up to the black Buick Rivera, and after opening the driver's side door, the man encouraged her to get closer to the car. She stuck her head inside to scope out the area, and seeing Simon sitting in the passenger seat, Kaitlyn knew she'd made a huge mistake that would lead to trouble. Then the next few minutes spun out of control. Strong arms pulled her into the car, tied her hands and feet with a hemp-like rope, placed a strip of duct tape tightly across her mouth, and strapped her into the seatbelt in the backseat.

Kaitlyn watched in fear as the older gentlemen, which she surmised now was Steven Sharpe, climbed into the car, locked the doors, and started the car. Then Simon reached into the car through the open back window, and pulled her car keys out of her purse. How could she have been so careless to have let her guard down? I'm so sorry Tat, she thought. She worked to reign in her terror and keep a straight head, so she turned her attention to her attackers.

Steven lit his cigar, took a long pull, and blew a couple of rings in the air. He raised the edges of his mouth and sent his son a wicked smile. "Remember, boy, if the car gives you any trouble, let it know I'm carrying some precious cargo." He turned to face Kaitlyn and took another pull from the stub. "We wouldn't want to hurt this pretty little thing," he said, blowing the smoke toward her.

Kaitlyn moved her head to dodge the pungent stink. The smell was making her nauseous; she had to curb the urge to vomit. With her mouth covered, that image didn't paint a pretty picture.

Simon stepped out of the car. "I don't know why I have to drive the T-Bird. There's something not right with that car. It gives me the creeps, and that mutt is in there now."

"We went over this already. I want the girl, she has something I want, and I intend on getting it. Now go get into her car, times wasting."

Kaitlyn's thoughts were on Gina. The top was still down, so maybe she'd get out. Kaitlyn prayed he didn't harm her dog. 'Sorry, Gina baby, I should've paid attention to your soft growl. I know now it was a warning.'

She sat back and wished she could dissolve into the seat. She tried not to gag from the stench of the disgusting car seat covers. She flinched when he reached behind and ripped off the duct tape from her mouth, and she opened it wide to stretch the sticky skin.

"You can scream as loud as you want; no one is going to hear you," he said. Then Steven turned back around, put the car in drive and drove off the lot.

Kaitlyn glared at him with her angry eyes, "I wouldn't give you the satisfaction," she snapped and turned her head away.

Steven shot her a devilish grin from the rearview mirror. "Oh, a little spitfire. I see a lot of that sweet Tatiana in you. Poor little thing. I just wanted one kiss. But I was never good enough for her. All she was interested in were those rich preppy guys. The ones that had money, nice cars, and lived in big houses."

Kaitlyn tried not to look his way. Out the corner of her eye, she could see him eyeing her through the rearview mirror. Her heart was breaking for the child, then and now.

Tatiana must ride in this nightmare again, and now Kaitlyn was being pulled into it. She hoped that the scared little spirit would open, show her fierce confidence, and let him know who was in control. The sound of a deep raspy voice brought her back to the present.

"Are you ok back there?"

"I'm fine." Kaitlyn curtly replied. She wasn't about to show him any fear. It was essential to connect to an unstable person on their level, so she had to stay focused and level-headed.

"You are such a pretty thing. I'm sorry you had to get mixed up in this. If you would've just given me what I wanted, we could've avoided all of this. Now I must take care of you myself. You understand, right?" he asked, watching her.

Kaitlyn nodded. She didn't want him to hear the shock in her voice. What was he going to do with her, and what did he want?

"You have it, right?" he asked and waited for her to answer.

Before Kaitlyn replied, she swallowed; disgusted by the taste of bile in her mouth. "I don't know what it is."

"Don't play dumb with me," he snapped, his loud voice echoing in the car.

Kaitlyn tried not to react; only this man was doing his best to scare her. It was apparent he had some mental problems. He could go from hot to cold and from Dr. Jekyll to Mr. Hyde within a sentence. She decided to keep a low profile and try not to upset him. "I don't have anything, but if you tell me what you're looking for, maybe I can help you find it," Kaitlyn said, offering a bargain.

"That is so nice of you," Steven replied. "You're one of the good ones. I just wish I didn't have to hurt you like her. It was a mistake, you know. I didn't want to hurt her. I just wanted one kiss."

Oh boy, Kaitlyn thought, I hope he doesn't ask me for a kiss. I'll spew all over him. No way was she kissing that gross, smelly mouth. This guy was certainly not firing on all cylinders. The sad thing was, he believed his lies. She just wanted to get away from this lunatic. She and her dad had a date at a car show tonight, and when she didn't show up, he'd trace her down. Her heart ached for Tatiana; she could imagine how scared and alone the child must've felt that night. Kaitlyn's anxious stomach, sick with the thought, was swirling in nervous acid. She took long, slow deep breaths; it was all she could do to keep from spewing out her insides. Hopefully, one of the millions of cameras Bill had placed around the yard had captured the kidnapping.

Kaitlyn looked out the window. It was dark, but there was just enough light for her to recognize her surroundings. She had an idea where he was taking her. And when they turned onto the gravel outlet, the number thirteen haunted her once again.

Steven parked the car, removed his seatbelt, and turned around to look at Kaitlyn. "So, you can make this easy on both of us, give me the item, and then I'll dispose of you, quick and easy. Otherwise, it could be slow and excruciating."

Back to Mr. Hyde again, Kaitlyn thought, trying to develop a plan to stall for time. "So, let me get this straight, you're going to kill me no matter what happens. So why should I give you what you want?" Kaitlyn watched as the man's eyes grew wide and glassy.

"It was the last day of school; I asked her to go steady and slipped my high school ring on her finger. I thought then that I would be worthy of a kiss. But she looked at me with disgust, glaring into my soul, like I was a piece of trash, she spit in my face and I lunged for the knife. Within seconds she was lying in my arms, my clothes covered in her warm blood. I didn't mean to do it," he confessed as tears cascaded down his face. "I loved her. But the little tramp still deserved it."

The words "sharp knife of a short life" and "kiss me deadly" rang through Kaitlyn's mind. Tatiana's musical lyrics were coming to life, only this time she was the co-star in this nightmare. Her heart pounded with panic. She could imagine how scared and alone Tatiana must've felt that night. This crazy man had stabbed her. Kaitlyn's anxious stomach, ill with the thought, was swirling. She took long, slow deep breaths as she thought about her situation. Maybe playing on his sympathy would buy her more time. She forced her eyes to soften, found a calm tone in her shaky voice, and then spoke softly. "I'm sorry. Maybe she wasn't aware of how you felt. Sometimes we girls do the craziest things without thinking, especially in our teenage years. But it doesn't mean we don't care."

"She didn't like me," Steven remarked. "You're not supposed to be mean to someone you care about. She made it quite clear; I didn't belong in her perfect little world. Now, where is that good for nothin' son of mine? He should've been here by now. That car better not have taken him on a detour. Cause if it did, you will pay."

OMG, back to Mr. Hyde again, Kaitlyn thought. She hoped Tatiana had veered him down some windy country road far away from here, but that hope washed away when headlights blinded her.

Steven walked over to the car and waited for his son to get out. "It's about time you got here. What did you do? Take the scenic route?"

"Don't blame it on me," Simon said, getting out of the car with his arms raised in his defense. "That crazy car tried to take control and turned off onto some side road. I did what you said, and she immediately broke the hold on the steering wheel. I'll tell you, that's some wacked-up piece of work. Must be a special computer chip inside it," he added, scratching his head with uncertainty. "Luckily that mangey dog jumped out, but it wasn't until after I poked at it with a stick."

Yes, her baby was safe, she celebrated in her mind. If she were hurt there would be hell to pay, she thought, feeling her anger rise.

Steven opened the back door with a long sharp knife held tightly in his hand. Here started the nightmare, she screamed in her head. The terrified hostage said a silent prayer; God, please send someone to help me.

14) COMING TOGETHER

Jason sat in the backseat of Bill's pickup; his heartbeat pounding hard in his chest. Rob and Bill took up the two seats in the front, debating over politics. Jason knew it was only a diversion to keep from going insane. They were on their way to rescue Kaitlyn, and the inside of the truck ran thick with anxious minds and hurting hearts. Ever since Jason had heard the news, he'd been overwhelmed with mixed emotions. Fear and anger were neck and neck for the lead. What riled him the most is he'd been so upset with her, and now that didn't matter. He just wanted her in his arms, safe and unharmed.

He had felt helpless as he'd watch the video and seen how Kaitlyn's assailants had lured her into the car. If only he'd been there. Luckily, her dad had put a tracer on her phone after the incident at the shop. Bill was driving at high speed, but it wasn't fast enough for Jason. He feared for her life, as everyone did in the truck. Every minute that passed gave her assailants another minute to hurt her. Oh God, please let her be ok, he said a silent prayer.

Kaitlyn walked in front of Simon, the dangerous delusional sociopath. The strong brave woman she'd grown into held her head high, kept quiet, took small steps, and trekked at a slow pace. However, the terrified inner child waved her hands frantically, screamed in terror, and wanted to run. But a sharp reminder, six inches from her back, held control of her fate. She'd have to harness that little child and obey his orders to stay alive. The eeriness covered her like a heavy blanket; something terrible had happened up here, she'd felt it then, and it was chasing her now. She took a deep breath and inhaled the clean country air and let the scent of pine and evergreen wash away the taste of the nasty cigar in her mouth.

Her legs shook with fear as she pulled together all the courage she had inside. But as Kaitlyn perused the area and took in her circumstances, she realized she didn't have a chance. She wouldn't get far with her feet and arms bound, and it was too dark to see her way around. Harrowing thoughts raced through her head. What if this was the end of her life? The news of her death would destroy her family. Just as Kaitlyn bowed her head in defeat and hugged her inner child, she felt a surge of energy go through her. She related the feeling to a static shock, only much more potent. What is happening? she asked herself.

"*Don't be afraid,*" a small voice spoke in her head.

"Who is this?" Kaitlyn asked the invader.

"*It's Tatiana,*" replied the voice.

Kaitlyn was confused. Really! Voices in her head. She wondered if there was a hallucinogenic on the tape that had covered her mouth.

"*We don't have a lot of time. We're going to have to pull together our strength, become one and outsmart these creeps.*"

Kaitlyn tried to remain calm. She didn't know what to think. How can this be? She could feel the strange presence in her but couldn't fathom the thought of something so inconceivable. Since that crazy car had come into her world, nothing had made sense. So why should this be any different? If it was normal, then she should worry. This thought made her giggle nervously. Seriously, the way it looked; she didn't have a lot of options. It looked like her fate was riding on merging with the entity inside her.

They came to a stop at the edge of the path. The light illuminated the cute little hill Kaitlyn had spotted when she and Jason had explored the area. Oh no, she screamed in her head as Tatiana revealed a picture of a body underneath the mound. Kaitlyn's body trembled; the words "darkness has kept the light concealed" stuck in her head. She swallowed deeply; her dry mouth yearned for water. She already knew the answer, but asked the creepy question anyway. "Is that you?"

"Yes, but don't freak; it's just a shell. I need you with a clear and calm head."

"I'll try," Kaitlyn responded as she watched Simon, who had appeared with a shovel and started digging in the dirt on the mound. She looked away and concentrated on her visitor. "How did you get so brave all of a sudden?"

"I couldn't let them do to you what they did to me. I stayed frozen in fear for too long. I decided it wasn't going to rule me anymore. I must've gotten angry enough to break the wall, and you were a safe body to join. We need each other."

"What is your plan?" Kaitlyn asked with a bit of apprehension.

"*I'm working on it.*"

Kaitlyn flinched as the hole grew deeper. "You'd better hurry because I have a feeling that hole is for us."

Simon laid his head on the shovel. "You think it is deep enough?" he asked his dad.

Steven took a shot from his flask. "Maybe just a little deeper. We don't want anyone finding her body." He walked over to Kaitlyn and grabbed her by the coat. "Come on. There's someone I'd like you to meet. I'm sure you two will get along fine." He pulled her toward the hole.

"*Wait!*" Kaitlyn pleaded, only it wasn't her. "*Stevie, why are you doing this? Untie me, and we'll go back into town. I want you as my date for the dance.*"

Steven's eyes grew dark, and he stepped back. "Only one person has called me that. What are you trying to pull?" he asked with suspicion.

"*Nothing,*" said a soft, calming voice. "*I realize I'd made a mistake. I've always wanted you, but I was so young and stupid. I'm deeply sorry. Untie me, Stevie, I want you to hold me. I'm yours; please help me find your ring.*"

Steven grabbed his head and yelled loudly. "Noooo.... You are making fun of me. How did you know that name, and where is the ring?"

"It's me, Tatiana; I've missed you, Stevie. Take this rope off me, and we can find it together."

"You're dead. I buried you over there," Steven said, pointing to the mound.

"I'm so disappointed that you don't recognize me," Tatiana said, throwing him a puppy face and toying with his affection.

Steven shook his head. "You're just trying to get into my head and confuse me." Then he stared deep into her eyes. "I can see inside your soul. How is that possible. What are you?" he asked, his eyes wide as he stepped away.

Kaitlyn took in the entire scene. It was like watching a movie. Only she was a participating player, more like a bystander. Tatiana was in control of her thoughts and movements. It was like being possessed, but the difference was she could take back control at any time.

The loud yell from Simon quieted the couple. "That's enough. I don't know what your game is, but the fun stops here. Dad, she's just messing with you. I don't plan to stay here all night. Let's get this over with, so we can go home."

Steven nodded. "You're right, son." He held out his hand to Kaitlyn, "Give me my ring."

Kaitlyn laughed, "And how am I supposed to do that? I'm a little tied up right now. Besides, I don't have it. It must be in the car."

Steven showed an evil smile. "Yes, it must be there. Well, if you don't have it, you're no use to me." He grabbed her arm and pushed Kaitlyn into the dark hole.

She landed face down, dirt filling her mouth and nose. She made her way to her knees and tried to spit out the moist earth. "Yech," she said quietly, and then a traumatizing thought struck her. "OMG, I know now, that song clue," Kaitlyn shrieked. "You were buried alive. We've got to get out of here," Kaitlyn said frantically, digging with her tied-upped hands.

Her hands brushed across a foreign object. She rolled it around in her hand. I think I found the ring. She squeezed it in her hand as though it was a lucky charm, thinking it could become a bargaining chip in exchange for her life.

"Keep a tight hold on that; you'll need it later," Tatiana stressed. *"Now feel around for a sharp rock. Maybe you can cut the rope tied around your hands. I'm going to slip out of your body and see what I can do up there. Hold on, Katie,"* Tatiana said as she detached from Kaitlyn.

Kaitlyn felt the energy leave her body, and the feeling left her weak, vulnerable, and scared. She only hoped that little spirit could overtake those men and she wanted to be prepared to help if Tatiana couldn't. Not wasting any time, Kaitlyn searched the dirt in hopes of finding a rock and praying Tat's bones didn't find her first. Luck was on her side, no bones, and a rock that felt like it might do the trick fell under her touch. Kaitlyn started rubbing the rope on the rough edge of the jagged rock. Boy, she was sure going to need a manicure when this over. She laughed nervously at the thought.

Kaitlyn tried to tune into the conversation going on above her, but the dirt muffled the sound a bit. What she could hear had her giggling, and it seemed as though Tatiana had everything under control.

"What are you doing, you crazy lunatic? Put that shovel down," Steven demanded.

"Believe me, dad, it's not me. Something has control over it," Simon replied as he moved closer to his father, the tool lifted above his head, ready to strike.

Steven ran to the nearest tree and stepped behind it to protect himself from his son. "I told you to put that shovel down. I warn you, boy," he threatened.

"I told you, dad. It's not me. There's something in my head," he answered, swinging the shovel while trying to get control. "I bet it has something to do with that strange car."

Meanwhile, the rock had worked like a charm. It had only taken a few minutes of intense rubbing on the rock to cut through the rope. After she freed her hands and feet, Kaitlyn put the ring in her pocket and climbed out of the hole. Keeping out of sight, she edged closer and looked on the scene.

Steven peeked around the tree and ducked to avoid being struck by the heavy instrument. His son charged at him, sending him running towards the hole. "You're crazy. You need some serious help, boy. Don't make me stab you with this knife." When he raised his arm to defend himself, Simon took a swing at his dad and caused him to fall backward, right into the hole and losing the knife in the process.

"Get me out of here," Steven screamed. A coughing fit had him gasping for air. "I need my inhaler. It's in the truck." He looked up in time to be bombarded by a shower of dirt. "What are you doing? You stop that right now, you hear." He attempted to move to the side of the hole as more dirt came into the hole.

Kaitlyn watched as Simon or Tatiana buried the choking man.

"What's going on here?" Bill said, appearing from the trail with a bright spotlight.

Kaitlyn spotted Jason and ran into his arms. "Oh Jason," she cried out, holding him tight.

"You're ok now, baby," he assured her, wrapping her tight in his arms. "What is happening over there?"

"Well, you wouldn't believe it if I told you," she whispered.

Kaitlyn heard her dad's voice and looked up to see him walking towards Simon. "Put down that shovel, son."

Simon stopped what he was doing and stood dumbfounded at the mercy of the two men. "I would if I could." And in mid-sentence, the shovel fell to the ground, and Bill and Rob grabbed the man.

"My father, he's buried down there. I didn't do it. Something had control of me," Simon stated, his eyes locked in a confused stare.

"Sure, you didn't do it," Bill commented in a calm condescending voice. "Here, you handle this garbage," he said to Rob as he passed the guy onto him. "I guess I should dig up the other piece of trash."

"Are you ok?" Jason asked, checking Kaitlyn's body for any signs of abuse.

"I'm fine, except for the rope burn on my ankles and wrists," Kaitlyn said rubbing her wrist. "I could use some water," she said grinding the dirt in her teeth. She jumped as the familiar energy plunged into her, and she could feel it retaking control. She was too tired to overpower the entity.

"*Hi Jason,*" Tatiana said in a pleasant voice.

"Uh hi," he replied, giving her a weird look as he handed her the water. "I think we should get you to the doctor. I have a feeling you could be in shock."

"*Nonsense, I've never felt better. How about a kiss?*" Tatiana asked, leaning closer to Jason.

Suddenly she was jerked back by Kaitlyn. "No kisses," she told Tatiana.

"*You're no fun,*" Tatiana said with a laugh. "*Alright, I promise to be good.*"

"Kaitlyn, what's going on with your body?" Jason asked, pulling her close.

Tatiana stepped back. "*It's not Kaitlyn. Well, it's her body, but I have temporary control of her now. It's me, Tatiana.*"

"Were you hit on the head?" Jason asked, his hand scanning her head.

"*No, she wasn't. Please don't be alarmed. I'm sorry about your dad. He was just trying to help me, but he got too involved, and they found out. I couldn't get to him in time.*"

"What are you talking about?" Jason asked, feeling anxious. "Kaitlyn, you're scaring me."

"*Jason, look into my eyes, and you'll see.*"

"Ok, but you're acting too strange." But all it took was one look, and Jason could tell there was something different; Kaitlyn's eyes were no longer blue and seemed vacant. Jason shook his head. "How can this be?" he asked. Just then, the sound of sirens broke the connection and gave Kaitlyn control. Jason stared into the loving eyes he knew and asked, "Where did she go?"

Kaitlyn smiled and took his arm. "Don't worry, she'll be back; I have a feeling her work here isn't done."

"I'm so confused," Jason confessed but moved on from the thought as they walked towards the officers. "Those two guys could use your help over there," Jason instructed, pointing to the hole. "That man that my uncle is holding, and the one buried in the dirt, abducted my girlfriend."

The officer tilted his head, trying to grasp onto the situation.

"Don't even try and figure it out," Jason said shaking his head.

"Are you ok to give a statement?" the officer asked Kaitlyn.

"I'm fine, and sure, whatever you need. Oh, by the way, you'll find the bones of a girl missing years ago at the bottom of the hole. Her name is Tatiana."

"Interesting. Well, Officer King can assist you with your statement. I'm going to find out what's going on over there."

Kaitlyn told her story to the officer, leaving out the part about the spirit. When she was finished giving her testimony, she leaned up against Jason. The evening had taken a toll on her, and this day couldn't end soon enough. She and Jason stepped out of the way as the officers passed by with her assailants. Simon was pleading his victim status and Steven, covered in dirt, cursed his son and the world. Kaitlyn shivered and moved closer to Jason when Steven's evil stare zeroed in on her.

"It's ok," Jason said, rubbing her arms. "You're safe with me, baby."

Within moments her dad and Bill were close by her side. And then the tears started flowing, and her body shook when Kaitlyn fell into her dad's arms. Jason's embrace had been comforting and soothing. But there wasn't anything that compared to her dad's safe and nurturing hug. Tonight, she had needed both.

"Ready to go?" Jason asked, urging Kaitlyn to move. He wanted to get her away from this horrible place.

Kaitlyn kissed her dad on the cheek, hugged Bill, grabbed Jason's hand, and walked down the trail. She hadn't felt Tatiana inside her. However, there hadn't been any energy surges, which led Kaitlyn to believe the entity was still there, hiding in the shadows of her soul.

When they reached her car, Kaitlyn hesitated before getting in. "He was in there," she said, frozen in place.

15) THE RING

Jason looked at the weary girl by his side and wished he could erase the night and make everything right for her again. However, he knew that was beyond his power and out of his control. The best he could do was be there for her, which he planned to do. Jason took her hand in his and said, "I'm sorry, baby. It's still Tatiana, and something tells me he didn't tarnish her. But if you'd feel more comfortable, you can ride back with Bill, and I'll take this girl home."

Kaitlyn didn't know how she felt. Simon had invaded her space; his presence had polluted the air and his creepy fingerprints, invisible to the eye, tainted the inside. The haunting memory would forever be tied to the driver's seat behind the wheel. But there was Jason; she needed to be close to him. He was right; nothing could break the spirit of that car. Tatiana had shown bravery and saved Kaitlyn's life. She could do the same, pull in her courage, and ride in the car. "I want to go with you. And thank you for coming here. I was so scared," Kaitlyn confessed as she broke down in his arms.

Jason held the trembling girl tightly. His fingers raked through her hair. "Not bad for an annoying sidekick, huh?" he joked, trying to lighten the moment.

Kaitlyn looked up, and with a smile peering through her tears, she replied, "An annoyance I'm falling in love with."

Jason was taken back by her words. They should've scared him, but they didn't. He was just overtaken by her admission. Some time ago, he'd fallen for her, but the grief from the loss of his dad had kept the truth hidden. After almost losing her tonight, his heart had opened, pushing away any doubts, and let her in. Jason gazed lovingly into Kaitlyn's beautiful teary eyes and professed his feelings, "I love you too." With that, they celebrated with a kiss.

As much as he would've loved to continue kissing Kaitlyn's delectable lips and sink into the sensual moment, he knew that it wasn't the right time and place. So, he gently pulled away. "Now, let's get you home," he said, opening the passenger door.

Under protest, Kaitlyn moved toward the car. She didn't want their passionate moment to end. It felt right and took her away from thoughts of her terrifying experience. And she didn't want to get into the car, but she took a deep breath and let Jason help her in.

Kaitlyn sat in the seat and turned up her nose. "Yech, it stinks. The creep was smoking in here," she said, covering her face.

"We can roll down the windows, and here, bundle up in my coat to keep warm. Tomorrow I'll make an appointment to have the entire car detailed inside and out. Let's get out of this eerie place."

Kaitlyn wrapped herself up in the coat and looked out into the night. The illuminating glow of the full moon cast ghostly shadows in the dark forest. Why was this area still haunting her? Shouldn't she feel peace? Wasn't there any closure? She also still wondered what had happened to Jason's father, and would they ever know?

"*There's still more to this story,*" said a little voice in her head.

"Tatiana, you're back," Kaitlyn said to the spirit in her mind.

"*I never left. Do you still have the ring?*"

"Yes. It's safe in here," she replied, feeling in her pocket for the object.

"*Good. Don't lose it.*"

"What's so important about this ring?" Kaitlyn asked, her curiosity growing.

"*I'll tell you tomorrow. You've had a traumatizing experience, and you need rest.*"

Kaitlyn had no strength left in her to debate with the spirit, so she laid her head against the door and closed her eyes. "Thank you, Tat," she said aloud as she dozed off.

It felt like she'd just fallen asleep when the sound of Jason's voice called to her. "Kaitlyn sweetie, we're home," he said as he rocked her gently.

She sat up; her head filled with fog. "What?"

"We're home," he said, meeting her at the passenger door.

Kaitlyn took his offered arm and got out of the car. Then a scary thought occurred to her. "Gina, she's still at the shop. We have to go back," Kaitlyn screamed.

Jason pulled her away from the car. "Look," he said, pointing to the excited pup running towards her.

Kaitlyn fell to the ground and threw her arms around her fur baby. "How, when?" she asked, letting the dog smother her with kisses.

Jason joined Kaitlyn and ruffled Gina's fur. The wild, wiry pup tossed her body around, causing him to laugh. "Bill brought her to your parents, and your dad must've dropped her off here a few minutes ago."

"I should've listened to your warning girl. I'll never doubt you again." she said, hugging her pup's neck and examining every inch of her body, relieved when there weren't any visible marks.

"You ready to go in?"

"Will you stay with me?" Kaitlyn asked with pleading eyes. "I'd rather not be alone tonight."
Jason showed a caring smile. "Sure, I'd planned on it. You going to tell me what went on up there?"

"Tomorrow," she said, then walked into her house.

Jason went directly to the bathroom while Kaitlyn plopped down on the couch with Gina close by her side. The picture of her and Brian caught her attention. She rose from her comfy seat and removed the memory from her wall. It was time to retire that phase of her life and replace it with new beginnings. Relieved and happy with her decision, she found her place on the couch, placed her head on the pillow, and was out like a light. Kaitlyn didn't feel Jason cover her with a blanket and curl up next to her.

The next morning Kaitlyn was awakened by the smell of bacon and a cold nose on her face. She stretched out on the sofa and then brought her sleepy self to life. The events of the previous night slammed into her like a swing from a wrecking ball. The memory temporarily took her hostage. She hugged herself to ward off a trembling chill.

"It's ok. You're safe, and everything is right again," Tatiana said, breaking into Kaitlyn's thoughts.

"Morning, I think," Kaitlyn greeted Tat. "You plan on taking up permanent residency in my head? If so, I'm going to start charging rent." She giggled. "Why are you still here? The mystery is solved; we caught Mr. Sharpe and his son. Shouldn't you be moving on to the next plane, Heaven or somewhere above the clouds?"

"I'm not sure, but it could be because there's more to this mystery. You found me. Now it's time to help you find Jason's dad."

That comment caused Kaitlyn's skin to crawl. Digging around in the dirt, looking for bones, made her physically ill. She'd had her share of terrorizing moments in the last twenty-four hours to last her a lifetime. The thought of needing therapy flashed through her mind. She laughed at her thought, but also knew there was truth to it as well.

"All three of us need to talk," Tatiana insisted.

Kaitlyn yawned. "Can't it wait until after we eat, and I've had... let's say about a dozen cups of coffee?"

Tatiana giggled. *"Sure, but remember time is precious,"* she stressed.

"Got it," Kaitlyn said, giving a thumbs-up. "Right now, my sights are on a handsome cook and food." Kaitlyn freshened up and then went to join him. She slipped behind him and wrapped her arms around his waist. "Morning," she said, nibbling his ear.

Jason turned away from the stove and drew her into his arms. "Morning, beautiful." Then he found her lips with his, savoring the welcoming greeting as he pulled her in closer, then went back to his cooking duties. "This is almost ready. You want to grab some plates and silverware?"
Kaitlyn gathered the items and set them each a place at the bar. "I didn't know you cooked," Kaitlyn said, taking a piece of bacon from the platter.

"I know my way around the kitchen and even have some recipes that would have your taste buds exploding. My mom taught me well."

"Well, I guess you're going to have to show me your stuff," Kaitlyn said, feeling a little flirty.

"Oh, don't worry, girl, I plan on it," he said with a wink.

Kaitlyn blushed and gave a shy smile.

"So, was that hard for you last night?" Jason asked, changing the subject.

Kaitlyn tilted her head, thinking that was a strange question. "Hard?" she asked with a confused look.

Jason pointed to the spot on the wall, where her and Brian's picture once shared the space.

Kaitlyn changed her thinking gears. "No, not really. I believe it was there to make me feel complete. Maybe at one time, I thought by having that picture there it would bring him back. Silly, I know," she stated.

"Not at all. I can think of another couple that would fit perfectly in that spot," Jason said with a sly smile.

"I think you're right," Kaitlyn agreed as she reached out and touched his hand.

"Before I forget, your mom and dad called. I told them you needed to sleep, and you'd call them later. They sounded overly concerned. I let them know you were safe. I hope they didn't get the wrong idea about why I was here."

"Thank you. It's none of their business who I have over," Kaitlyn said, putting on an I don't care façade on the outside. "I'll explain it was all innocent," she added, deciding it was better to erase the picture painted in their minds. It was up to her what she did but keeping it low-key and not advertising her intentions was the best plan of action with her parents.

"*It's time, Sis,*" Tatiana strongly stated.

"You sure are a pest." Kaitlyn formed an ear-to-ear grin. "Is that why you gave me so much trouble. You viewed me as a big sister?"

"Uh-huh, you were fun to tease. You were so wet and so mad when I took you through the irrigation sprinklers. But it got you into Jason's clothes." She smirked.

"Did I say something funny?" Jason asked, following the reaction on her face.

"No. Tatiana is back in my head. It seems she never left."

Jason flashed a frown. "Why is she inside you and not the car? I'm still having a rough time understanding all of this."

Gina then gave a loud bark, tilting her head from side to side as she stared strangely at her master.

"I think your dog agrees with me," Jason added.

"I'm sorry, baby," Kaitlyn said, bending down to pet her faithful furry companion. Then she looked up at Jason. "Tatiana says it's lonely out there. And she wants to talk with us. So, in a couple of minutes, I'm going to let her have control. Remember, it's not me. That means no touchy or kissy. Understand?" Kaitlyn asked, more for Tatiana's sake.

"Got it," Jason answered as he put the last bite of bacon in his mouth.

"She first wants me to put Steven's ring on the table." Kaitlyn sat up, reached into her pocket, pulled out the dirt-covered gold band, and washed it off before placing it between herself and Jason.

Jason picked up the ring and inspected it. "There's writing on the inside."

"What does it say?" curious eyes moved closer.

He squinted his eyes. "It's hard to make out, but I'll try," he said, reading the inscription. "My love for eternity, Sar..." and he suddenly stopped dead. The tinging sound of the ring hitting the table as it slipped through his fingers, rang in the silence.

"What's wrong, Jason?" Kaitlyn asked, seeing the spooked expression on his face. Jason said, "This ring doesn't belong to Steven; it's my dad's. My parents had this blessing written in their wedding rings. Where did you find it? And where did the blood come from?" he asked with a baffled look.

Kaitlyn picked up the ring and swallowed before divulging the information. She didn't want to say, but he had to know so that he could find closure. She wished it weren't her that had to break his heart. "It was buried in the ground with Tatiana."

"Noooo..., it can't be," Jason yelled out. "I thought Serena said he was alive."

"Jason, I told you that wasn't a for sure thing; that's why I was hesitant to tell you," she said, reaching for his hand. The next moment a powerful source inside her mind pushed Kaitlyn away and took over. *"Let me take it from here."*
"Jason, it's me, Tatiana. Let me tell you what happened to your father. Like you and Kaitlyn, he learned about the mystery and wanted to help. Of course, I sent him the same clues, which led him to Milepost Thirteen, to the exact location. Steven thought the ring your dad was wearing was his and forced him to give it up. He scraped

his finger as he ripped it off him. That's where the spot of blood came from. He made his son dig in the same hole where he buried me. He planned to bury your father there."

"I don't want to believe this," Jason cried out, resting his head in his hands. "He's there with you, isn't he, in the ground?"

Tatiana took hold of Jason's hand and squeezed it tight. *"Let me finish. I couldn't help the way I did last night. All I could do was sit back and helplessly observe the horror. I know now fear had me trapped. I cried inside for Greg. We had become good friends. Your dad is a good man."*

"You mean was," Jason said, covering an escaped tear.

Tatiana smiled, *"No, I mean, 'is.' As far as I know, he's still alive."*

"What? How can that be?" Jason jumped up with enthusiasm. "Did he dig his way out?"

"Greg moved out of the way when Steven tried to shove him in the hole. Taking the only way out, he hobbled with great speed and jumped off the cliff. After realizing the ring wasn't his, Steven tossed it in the hole."

Jason thought for a moment. Then a memory hit him. "I was right. That was his flannel. Can you bring Kaitlyn back for a couple of minutes? I want to share all this with her."

"I can, but she already knows."

"This is nuts," Kaitlyn commented. "'I'm so happy for you," she said, doing a happy dance with glee as she wrapped her arms around his neck.

"*Hey guys,*" remarked the little spirit, who stepped back from Jason and continued the saga. "*I hate to spoil your celebration, but we still have work to do.*"

"Ok, so what do we do? Where is he?" Jason asked, excitedly tossing out questions.

Tatiana placed her hand against her face in an l shape and gave a heavy sigh. "*Well, I don't know exactly where he is. That, I'm leaving in your hands.*"

"What, no musical clue?" Jason asked with a sarcastic tone.

Tatiana swatted her hand like she was shooing away a fly. "*For your information, I did leave one.*"
"Which one?" Kaitlyn asked. "*I played a song the night you were in Astoria. You and Serena were in the car. Katie you immediately turned it off. I couldn't find the song again in time. I had to search through a long list to find the right songs with the right words. It was the only way I had to communicate. That was until I found my own voice and pulled myself out of the shadow of fear.*"

"So, what happened to my dad?" Jason asked, getting anxious.

"*Well, he wasn't dead, like his attackers had assumed. I had also given up hope, but he appeared at the top of the hill after a while. His head was bleeding, and the blood had stained the torn flannel, which was barely hanging on his shoulders. I could tell he was disoriented as his steps*

were in a zig-zag pattern. He made it to the shoulder of the main street and fell to the ground."
Tatiana paused for a moment, then walked over to the fridge and chose a diet soda. She popped the top and took a deep swig. *"Yum, this is so good. It's been years."* She examined the can. *"I almost forgot what it tastes like."* She took another drink and was about to finish her story when Kaitlyn chimed in.

"Are you about done? I want my body back," she commented.

"Yes, give me about five minutes. You have any pizza?"

"No, finish already," Kaitlyn demanded.

"Fine. You know you're not always fun."

"Kaitlyn," Jason called out.

"Huh? Yes, it's me. I'm sorry, Tatiana gets into my head, and I become oblivious to everything else." Kaitlyn placed a hand on each side of her head, stuck out her tongue, and shook her head. "Argh, I'm not sure which are my thoughts, and which are hers."

Jason pulled Kaitlyn into his arms. "This is you, right?" he asked, hesitant to get too close.

"Yes, I swear it's me, for a moment anyway. Kiss me before I become possessed." She opened her eyes wide and put her hands on the side of her face "Ohhhhh," Kaitlyn teased.

"Ha, ha," Jason said, stealing a kiss.

"Ok, guys, break it up. Let's get back to business. I'm sure I have places to go." Tatiana demanded.

"Could you warn me when you do that?" Jason asked, pulling away.

Tatiana giggled. *"What would be the fun in that? Anyway, back to that night. Someone in a pickup truck noticed Greg along the highway and stopped to investigate. A man got out and was able to help him up. Greg leaned against the man. I heard the man ask what his name was. Greg went silent and felt around for his wallet. When he couldn't find it, he told him it was Jason."*

"What? Why do you think he chose my name?"

"I wasn't sure at first, then I thought he might have had a concussion and didn't know who he was, and your name popped into his head."

"Where did the man take him?" Jason asked eagerly.

"I don't know. But I did get the license plate number of the car: JEN 309."

The numbers "86 75 309" and the name Jenny rang through Kaitlyn's mind. She remembered hearing those words from the radio and was a little upset with herself for tuning out the song. But she took her focus off the mishap and concentrated on their next move. "Ok, Tatiana, I want my body back," she voiced aloud.

"One second, and it's all yours," Tatiana replied, then turned her attention back to Jason. *"I think I've helped as much as I could. I hope you find your father. Please thank him for me,"* she expressed.

"You're not planning on riding this thing out?" Jason asked.

"Yeah, come along with us," Kaitlyn said, urging her along. Then Kaitlyn jerked as she felt the energy of the spirit exit her body. Again, it was physically and emotionally exhausting. "She's gone," Kaitlyn said, releasing a sigh.

"Where did she go?" Jason asked, looking around the room.

Kaitlyn shrugged. "I don't know, maybe back into the car. We can look for her later. She gave us the missing link. If we follow it, I believe it will lead us to your dad. Can you contact your friend at DMV and see if she can find out who owns the car?"

Jason, holding his phone in his hand, commented, "I'm already on it. I can't believe this. Mom is going to be so excited," he said with tears in his eyes.

Kaitlyn grabbed Jason's hand, a serious look in her eyes. "Don't you think we should wait to tell her until after we locate him? Just saying, we don't know what mental condition he's in."

"I guess," he replied with a heavy sigh. "Why don't I leave so you can get ready. I need to shower and change, so I'll be back. Say in about an hour. Hopefully, I'll have the information from my friend."

"Sounds good." With that, Kaitlyn lightly brushed his lips with hers. "Hurry back," she said with a flirtatious tone.

Jason cast a sly grin and said, "It will feel like I've never left."

16) GREG

Kaitlyn sat on the couch after Jason left. It had been a bizarre over-the-edge morning, and all she wanted to do was allow herself a few moments to regroup and put things into perspective. It wasn't 10:00 yet, and she'd already had a man crash into her heart and a spirit break into her mind. She wondered if anyone else was having this much fun before noon. And to top it off, the terrifying night in the forest still haunted her.

What seemed like a few minutes had turned into thirty. Kaitlyn was still tired and drained from yesterday. It was hard for her to get moving. Remembering she was still dressed in the dirty attire she wore last night gave her the motivation to get her butt in gear.

As she headed to her bathroom, she felt the garments needed to be sterilized or tossed away like the night. Sterilization was the better option; the outfit was one of her favorites.

Kaitlyn was almost ready when Jason pulled up. She had chosen her distressed blue jeans, gray hoodie, and laced up booties. Perfect road trip attire. She'd need a heavy coat and gloves for the cold. You never could tell what the weather would be over the mountain. They might even run into some snow.   Seeing the hot man at the door with two coffees in hand had her heart pumping and the butterflies inside tickling her stomach. There wasn't any chill in the air now.

"I could get used to this," she said with a glowing smile while accepting her cup. "You're spoiling me."

Jason returned her smile. "As it should be. Besides, I figured you'd need the extra boost of caffeine after last night and this morning. I could tell you were dragging. My head is still spinning from what we learned today. It doesn't seem possible or real. Was I dreaming?"

"Well, if you were, we were both sharing the same dream," she commented as she rested her hand on his shoulder. "You ready to get this party started?"

"Ready as I'll ever be. My friend was able to locate the recent owner of the car, Michael Woods. However, he isn't the one who found my dad, and the address they have for the previous owner, Doug Wilson, is no longer valid. I spoke to Michael briefly and he said he bought the car about a year ago. He mentioned that Doug had been withdrawn and quiet, a man of few words. He doesn't know where he lives, but he thinks its somewhere out in the country outside of Sisters."

Kaitlyn twisted her lips to the side as she thought. "No address? What, are we going to just go there and search for him? It will be like looking for a needle in a haystack."

"I know it sounds like a long shot, but we can ask around. Maybe something will turn up. I must do this, with or without you. I prefer having you by my side."

Kaitlyn hesitated for a moment and then gave him an ear-to-ear grin. "As it should be," she replied repeating his quote. "Let me grab a coat, get Gina's leash and let's hit the road," Kaitlyn expressed with excitement.

"Michael said the owner mumbled a girl's name and said it sounded like Tatiana."

Kaitlyn smirked. "Boy that sassy little girl sure leaves a memorable impression," she said, trying to lift the shadow of despair hovering over Jason.

"She does at that," he said with a lopsided grin.

Kaitlyn could tell he was battling his emotions regarding the possible reunion with his father. She wished she had some words that could take the uncertainty away, or a touch that could make the pain disappear. The only thing she had to offer was encouragement, support, and prayers that it would all work out. Two years was a long time to be away from your family, and she wondered if they would find him. She held in a tear at the thought, as she called for her dog and locked up her house.

Kaitlyn looked at her car as she settled into the truck. It was like a hollow shell, a lifeless soul.

She wondered if Tatiana had ventured back into the safety of her metallic home. Her question was answered when the song lyrics "*Celebrate good times, come on*" flowed through the radio.

The couple looked at each other with surprised open mouths. "You've got to be kidding me," Jason expressed. Then they burst out in a peal of roaring laughter as he pulled out of her driveway.

"It really shouldn't be a big surprise. We should've expected it. Guess Tat wants to see how it all plays out. She was one of the main players in this strange mystery."

"Yeah, I suppose," Jason said with a little irritation in his tone.

"Besides, you have to admit her presence has lifted the sadness some. We have become a team, and it feels right having her here with us. And you should probably just succumb to it. I don't think you have a choice," Kaitlyn concluded with a shrug.

"Fine, but she'd better not mess with my radio or any of the accessories in my truck. You hear that missy?" he voiced to the spirit.

The sassy entity replied by making all the lights flash, the radio blast, and anything else she could activate.

"TATIANA!" Jason yelled.

Kaitlyn faced the window, a smile hidden on her face. She didn't want to be a contributor to the displeased look on his face. "Oh, Tatiana," she whispered in her head, as she felt the spirit transfer inside her.

"Thought he could use a good distraction," she said with a giggle.

Kaitlyn had Jason swing by her parents' house on their way out. She informed them they were going on a road trip to Sisters, leaving out the details, and hopefully would be back late that night. After promising her dad to keep in contact, they were free to get on the road. "Sheesh," Kaitlyn expressed with a heavy sigh walking to the car. "Is he ever going to see me as an independent woman? I'm not in any imminent danger anymore."

"You might as well get used to it," Jason said, taking her hand in his. "He's always going to worry about his little girl." Jason left it at that. He knew how much her dad loved and cared for her. After going through the nightmare of almost losing his daughter, Jason understood the unsettling emotions her dad was feeling. He wasn't the only one wanting to protect the precious gem. Jason would keep a watchful eye over her, making sure it was unnoticed and he stayed under her radar.

It wasn't long before they were driving up the foothills along the flowing Santiam River, and up to the mountain pass. Kaitlyn never grew tired of this drive. She loved the lush Douglas fir and red cedar forest trees that created the scenic corridor. She had traveled these roads on many of their family vacations. As she passed by some of her favorite spots, memories waved at her from the top of the mountains, the quaint little tourist towns, and breathtaking lookouts. She only hoped this quest would be an addition to her precious memories. Kaitlyn could sense the mystery was keeping them all in suspense and feeling anxious. They played silly car games to keep down the tension, kept topics light and simple, and stayed in the present moment. They decided to park any thoughts of what might-be or could-be in an empty car lot until they arrived at their destination.

Kaitlyn talked to Jason about stopping at her favorite eatery in Sisters, a must-do tradition that started in her early childhood. As usual, she chose the Saloon Burger, and Jason tried his luck with the Bison Burger. They ate their meal at a table next to the window so they could people watch and check out the mountaineer's city.

Under normal circumstances, it would've been a perfect date outing. But Kaitlyn knew all romantic notions would have to be put on hold until the last clue was unlocked, allowing Tatiana to move on. However, something told Kaitlyn it wasn't going to be easy, especially when the person holding the key may not have memories of what happened.

Before they left the diner, a cheery young hostess refilled their drinks in to-go cups. She froze in place while handing them to Jason. "You look familiar. Have you been in here before?" she asked, intensely checking him out.

Jason gave a pleasant smile and replied. "This is my first time here. That happens a lot. I guess I have one of those faces."

"It's those eyes. I've seen them somewhere before." She thought for a second, then snapped her fingers. "I know now. There is a guy staying at my grandpa's cottage and I could swear he has those same eyes."

Jason faced Kaitlyn with his hands in his pocket. "You think that could be my dad?" he asked.

Kaitlyn shrugged. "It's something we can look into. Maybe this is the needle we're looking for."

"What can you tell me?" he asked, his attention back to the waitress.

The waitress stepped aside from the cash register and assisted Jason and Kaitlyn over to a little table, where she urged them to sit. "Two years ago, this man came to live with my grandpa. Well, he really is just a good friend that we call grandpa. Have for years. He just showed up there one day. He told me the guy's name was Jason, and he hired him as a handyman."

Jason put his head in his hands and brushed them through his hair. "My dad went missing two years ago, and he's been there all this time, and nobody knew."

The waitress reached out and touched his arm. "I didn't know," she expressed with sympathy. "Grandpa has been very distant and lonely ever since Grandma passed on. I don't go out there as much as I should. When I do, your dad Jason is always working."

"Greg, my dad's name is Greg. My name is Jason, and this is my girlfriend, Kaitlyn. Is it possible to get the address?"

The waitress smiled and said, "Nice to meet you both. I'm Vickie, and I can do better than give you the address. My shift ends in about fifteen minutes, and I can escort you out there. Grandpa's pretty attached to that handyman, and I should be there when you take your dad home. I have a feeling it will break his heart. Got to go. Catch you in a few," Vickie said as she stood to leave as an arriving customer entered through the door.

"Thank you. We'll be waiting in the car," Jason commented, then laid his arm against Kaitlyn's back.

Outside Kaitlyn walked with a bounce. "Wow, what are the chances that we'd find the location of your dad so easy? It was dropped into our lap."

She put her hand in his and gazed into his fragile stare. "Are you ok in there?"

Jason looked down at his feet and kicked a small rock. "I don't know. I've prayed every day for this time. What if my dad doesn't recognize me or will never know I'm his son? What about mom? They were so much in love. Will they ever find it again?"

Kaitlyn raised his chin with her hand and brushed a stray hair from his eye. She searched in his sad eyes. "Jason, I don't know the answers to those questions. I wish I did. There are many medical procedures and doctors trained to deal with amnesia. Let's have hope and a lot of faith that he can recover. Right now, be happy he's alive and you know you will see him today."

"You're right," he said, relaxing his raised shoulders and pulling her into a hug. "I couldn't have done this without you."

Kaitlyn took his hand as they walked to the car. "I'm glad to be here with you, and everything is going to be ok. Let's sit in the truck where it's warm and rest for a few minutes. The events of last night are still wearing on me."

Twenty minutes later, Kaitlyn awoke to the sound of Vickie tapping on her window. She rubbed her drowsy eyes, rolled down the window, and twisted her nose when a waft of cigarette stink leaked in.

"Hey guys, I'm sorry it took me so long. A large family showed up after you left. I couldn't leave until after I'd served them. I must warn you. It's a gnarly drive up a steep gravel road. There are a few dangerous curves and steep embankments and one brutal switchback, but besides that you'll find a beautiful view of the mountains. Heaven help us, though, if one of the locals up there decides to drive into town. The road is barely wide enough for one car. I'll drive slowly to avoid you having to eat my dust."

Jason stretched his long legs and smoothed back his hair with his hand. "We're right behind you." With that, he settled into the driving position and pulled up behind Vickie's truck, ready to start the last leg of their journey.

The drive started on blacktop, where they followed a babbling stream which led to a roaring fast-flowing creek. The trip took a dramatic twist when the luscious forest terrain changed to desert-like country, where much of the landscape was tainted by forest fires, leaving blackened grounds and bare trees. When they hit the large-pebbled gravel and started climbing, their pace slowed significantly. Kaitlyn looked over at Jason as the truck rocked along. His hands were wrapped tightly around the steering wheel, and his gaze was locked on his surroundings. She could feel the tension in the truck. Not even Tatiana's upbeat musical attempts could cut through his emotional turmoil. There wasn't any more she could say or do. He would have to battle and conquer his inner fears on his own.

"Vickie wasn't exaggerating about this road," Jason spoke, pulling Kaitlyn out of her thoughts. "That's a long way down," he expressed, quickly glancing over the side.

"I'll take your word for it," Kaitlyn answered, looking the other direction. "Good thing I used the ladies' room before we left," she laughed nervously, trying to add some lightness to the anxiety-filled environment in the truck.

Finally, after what seemed like a never-ending climb up a steep hill, they came to a stop. A large metal gate securely locked with a no trespassing sign attached prevented them from traveling any further. After Vickie removed the lock and opened the heavy gate, she approached their truck.

"Please don't be too hard on my grandfather. The family suspects he may have the onset of Alzheimer's. He's too stubborn to see a doctor. He lost his son, Rick, five years ago, and it's been two years since my grandmother's passing." Vickie took a moment to compose her emotions before continuing. "If that wasn't hard enough for our family, many years back he lost his great granddaughter, who he never got a chance to meet, in the Silver Falls area. The authorities never found her. That was when the first pieces of his heart started to fall. All the deaths broke down a strong and sharp-minded man. He used to be so alive, witty, and quite adventurous. Now he just stays hidden up here in the middle of nowhere and talks to very few people."

Kaitlyn and Jason looked at each other in amazement. Both were thinking the same thing as they blurted out, "Was his great granddaughter's name Tatiana?"

"Yes," Vickie said, grabbing onto the truck mirror to keep from falling over from the shock. "How could you possibly know that?" she asked, her eyes wide with wonder.

"It's a long story, one for the books, that's for sure," Jason said, his mind still reeling from the news. "I'll fill you in later, but right now, I want to see my dad."

"Sure," Vickie said as her shaking hands reached in the pocket of her flannel for a cigarette.

"*I have a great grandfather,*" Tatiana yelled inside Kaitlyn's head. "*You've got to let me hug him. Pleeease?*" she begged.

"Of course," Kaitlyn answered, still processing the news herself.

Kaitlyn turned to Jason and asked, "How can this be possible? My head is spinning right now. Not to mention the gravel dance we endured for the last thirteen miles has played havoc on my bladder." She admitted. Then she realized that the number thirteen had been a sign of good luck this time. Her first reaction was to tell Jason, but judging by the stoic look on his face, she figured it would be a story best left for another time.

Jason inhaled and exhaled deeply as he drove through the gate. The rhythm of soft blues playing on the radio filled the silence of his swirling, mixed-up thoughts. He still couldn't get over the idea that his dad had been living here for two years with Tatiana's great grandfather.

Two souls together, leaning on each other. It made him wonder if this was a plan from a higher power. It was too deep a thought for him to dive into right now. None of that mattered now. He had found his dad, and he couldn't wait to see him. Excitement and uncertainty hung in the air when he parked the truck.

Kaitlyn and Jason sat in the truck while Vickie explained the situation to her grandfather. She tried to ignore the little singing voice, playing over and over in her mind. "*I get to see my great grandpa; I get to see my great grandpa.*"

"Really, Tat," Kaitlyn replied, mentally blocking the noise as she took in her surroundings. Directly in front of her was a large log cabin; smoke billowed from the chimney.

To the left of the house stood a large chopping block, outside a metal shed, which she surmised held the wood for the long winter's chilly nights. On the other side was a red barn, where horses leaned their heads over a wooden fence to greet the new arrivals. She could hear chickens cackling at a coop nearby. "Your dad's been living here for years. It looks like a good environment. At least he was safe, warm and by the size of those heifers in the field," she pointed to a herd of cattle behind the cabin, "they've been eating well." She laughed, breaking the ice.

Jason started to reply, but his jaw dropped as he saw his dad approach Doug, Vickie's grandfather. "I want to run up there and hug him. Only I'm afraid he won't remember me," he said with disappointment.

Kaitlyn could sense his hesitation and his inability to move. "Let's walk up to him slowly." She tugged on his arm to get out of the truck.

Jason held tight to Kaitlyn's hand. The last time he'd been this scared, was when he was told his dad was missing. In his heart, when he saw the confused look on this man's face, Jason knew his dad's body was there, but his mind was still missing.

"Grandpa, this is Jason and Kaitlyn. They're friends of mine," Vickie said, setting the scene.

"Hi, glad to meet you. Any friend of Vickie's is a friend of mine," he said, holding out his hand.

Jason took the man's large and fragile hand and accepted his handshake. "Thanks, you have an incredible place here."

"Yeah, not bad," Doug answered proudly, surveying his land.

Doug turned to greet Kaitlyn. They were all surprised when she threw her arms around his neck and hugged him tightly. Then she was shocked when the words *"I love you, great grandpa,"* came out of her mouth. "No, no, no, Tatiana," Kaitlyn screamed in anger at the spirit in her head. "What do you think you are doing? You said you wanted to hug him, not give him a heart attack."

"Sorry, I got caught up in the moment," Tat said with a sly apology.

"Excuse me," Doug said with a bewildered expression.

Kaitlyn stepped back, her hand over her reddened face. "You remind me of my grandfather, and I let my emotions run away." She cleared her throat and said, "Ahh, could I please use your ladies' room? Long bumpy ride," and she giggled as she headed to the house away from the awkward situation.

"Good save," Tatiana said with a laugh.

"I'm not speaking to you," Kaitlyn said in a tone of frustration.

"Ahh... come on, I apologized. I promise to be good."

Kaitlyn didn't answer while she made her way through the cabin. She was impressed by how clean it was, and she imagined the country flair and furniture décor was all Vickie's doing. It did create a comfy and welcoming appeal in the homey cabin.

Kaitlyn returned just as Doug was introducing Greg to his son. "This is my friend and live-in handyman, Jason."

At first, hearing his name shook him up a bit, but he contained himself. He wasn't sure whether to hug him or shake hands. The decision was made for him as his father pulled him in for a hug. "I love you, dad," Jason quietly whispered in his ear.

Greg pulled away, rubbed his eyes, and cradled his head in his hands. Then he looked up and stared into eyes like his own. "Do I know you from somewhere? You look familiar. Do you live nearby?" Greg asked.

"No, I live in Stayton," Jason answered.

"Then how would I know you?" he asked, taking a seat on the porch.

Jason wasn't sure how to answer that question. He didn't want to frighten the man. But how was he going to get him to believe and trust him? Had his dad heard him profess his love, or had it got lost in his head?

Kaitlyn saw the harrowing look on Jason's face and stepped in. She went up to Greg and introduced herself and greeted him with a loving hug. She was at a loss for words as he let go of her. She had no idea how to play this out, so she decided it was better to stay with what was familiar for him. "So, how long have you lived up here in his beautiful country?"

Greg scratched his head. "I think about two years now," he said, waiting for a verifying nod from Doug.

"I was looking for a job in town and happened to stumble across this great man," he said with a smile as he threw his arm over Doug's shoulder. "He offered me a job and a home."

Kaitlyn smiled back. "I can see why you'd take him up on his offer. It's so beautiful and serene up here. Where are you from?" Kaitlyn asked, keeping with the small talk but trying to advance things along.

"I'm not sure," Greg admitted. "I can only remember bits and pieces of my past life." Then he looked down at the ground and kicked a stone by his foot. "I've found a good life up here, but hopefully someday I will remember."

Vickie stepped close to her grandfather, "It's time, grandpa."

Doug coughed in his hand as he stalled for time. Kaitlyn felt sorry for the elderly gentlemen. She could tell this wasn't going to be easy for him or anybody else, for that matter.

Doug sat down next to Greg and paused for a moment before telling him everything. He apologized for not being completely honest. He admitted it was all with good intentions. Doug told him he felt connected to him the night he found him alongside the road, hurt and disoriented. He had planned to bring him to his home until he was healed and had his memory back. But days became weeks, and weeks became months, and they built a good friendship. He liked the extra help and companionship and couldn't bring himself to tell him the truth. He hoped that someday Greg could forgive him.

Greg jumped up. "No, this can't be. I don't know these people," he expressed, fear filling his eyes.

Doug rose and stood next to Greg with sadness wearing on his face. "You need to go with your family."

"You are my family."

"No, son, I'm a good friend with a feeble mind and weak body who didn't want to be alone."

"Well, I'm not leaving. There's too much left to do. What kind of a friend would I be to leave you with all this work?"

"What are we going to do?" Jason whispered to Kaitlyn.

Kaitlyn rolled her eyes as she deliberated, then raised her finger as a thought crossed her mind. "Not we, Jason. What can *she* do? Tat?" she called out to her spiritual friend. "Can you make a more profound connection with him?"

"Move over, sister, I'm already on it," Tatiana said, filling in and taking control of Kaitlyn.

Kaitlyn slipped her arm in Greg's. *"It's me, Tatiana. Walk with me a bit."*

"What?" he answered. "I thought your name was Kaitlyn. However, that name does sound familiar. Why is that?" he asked, staring bewilderedly at the young girl on his arm.

"It's a long story, and it would only add to your confusion. I was a friend you tried to help, which caused you to end up here. Now it's my turn to help you. I know you don't understand or recognize me, but that is your son. He has risked his life to find you and learn the truth about me," Tatiana said as they walked over to horses. *"He continued your mission. I need you to trust me. Can you do that?"*

"How do I know this is not a scam? You'll lure me away from the old man and then attack and rob him when he's alone," Greg asked with concern.

Tatiana turned to Greg. *"I can see how all of this could look suspicious. It even looks bad from where I'm standing. Just promise me to do one thing."*

"What's that?"

"Really gaze into Jason's eyes, your son's. I think you'll see that I'm telling you the truth. We need to go back. I feel myself getting a little lightheaded," Tat said.

"What's going on?" Kaitlyn asked Tat. "I feel you slipping away."

"I think I'm through here. My tasks are done for now. I found my great grandfather and reached out to Greg. It's time for me to move on. That's why you're feeling a little dizzy and weak, I'm slipping away. Kaitlyn, walk Greg back to his son. I believe he's ready to go."

Kaitlyn did as Tatiana asked. They walked back like two robots. He didn't say a word. Kaitlyn could tell by the worry lines on his face that he was trying to put the pieces together in his already mixed-up mind. She wished she could help the man, who might someday be her father-in-law. That was a strange thought to pop into her head.

When they returned to the group Greg made his way over to Jason and looked deep into his eyes. "You do have my eyes," he said, studying the boy. "I'm sorry I don't recognize you."

"That's ok," Jason said, holding in his emotions and wanting to pull his father in for a family reunion hug. However, it was too soon, and he felt the action might scare him away. Instead, he patted him on his back and said, "Let's go home and see mom."

"Mom?" Greg questioned.

"Yes, your wife Sara."

Greg froze in place. His eyes glassed over as he searched for the memory and he stared into the woods. "Sara, my sweet Sara."

Jason rushed to his side. "Do you remember her?" he asked with excited hope.

Greg cradled his head, shook it, and ran his fingers down his face. "I'm afraid only fragments. Before we go, I need to say good-bye to my friends."

Kaitlyn could no longer contain her tears, and by the time all the hugs and good-byes were passed around, she was a blubbering mess.

Jason laid his hand on his father's back and wrapped his arm around Kaitlyn's waist. "Let's go home." With that, they loaded into the truck. Before they left, Kaitlyn felt Tatiana's presence inside her again. *"Let me say good-bye to Jason. How about one kiss on the cheek?"*

Kaitlyn smiled and answered quietly, "Ok, but just one kiss on the cheek."

Tatiana leaned close to Jason and put her arms around his neck and searched his eyes.

"Hey, Tat," he said, as he gave her an endearing hug.

"You take care of our girl," Tatiana whispered in his ear. Then she kissed his cheek. He sensed she was gone when he felt Kaitlyn's lips on his. At least he hoped it was Kaitlyn kissing him. He pulled away and patted her knee.

Then he waved at Doug and Vickie as they headed out.

17) SIX MONTHS LATER

It was a beautiful day, perfect for a top-down, radio-blasting drive. Kaitlyn never passed up a day that welcomed the opportunity for a road-trip. Today, she was cruising in her best friend, Tatiana. Greg had let her keep the beautiful car. He laughed as she told him he'd have to pry her hands from the steering wheel if he didn't. Sunny was back to herself and running like a champ. Kaitlyn still loved her little bug. But sometimes wanted to feel the connection to Tatiana, and driving the Thunderbird gave her that closeness.

She headed out to her favorite spot in the country. A spiritual and peaceful place where she came to reflect and regroup. After turning into the gravel pullout, the realization hit her that the signpost, noting milepost 13, no longer haunted her. In fact, the number thirteen no longer posed any threat.

Kaitlyn walked down the short path to a small hill, bent down and placed a bouquet of roses next to the silver plaque. She brushed off the debris covering the lettering and read aloud, "Tatiana, may her spirit live on in our hearts." This was not her permanent place of rest. That was in a family graveyard, where a small service had taken place just weeks after the remains of her body were discovered and the family notified. This place here, however, was where Kaitlyn felt connected to her spirit friend. She sat cross-legged on the ground with Gina, who had a ball tucked inside her mouth, and updated Tatiana on the past months.

"Hey Tat. I'm sorry it's been so long since I've been here. Just a lot's happening in my life. Jason and I are still dating, and it's starting to get serious. I love him so much. I have a feeling he may ask me to marry him soon. He mentioned that the blank steppingstone at my parents, waiting to represent my family, needed to be filled in. This both excites and scares me. I wish you were here; I could sure use your courage. I'm weak when it comes to succumbing to a new relationship. It scares the hell out of me," Kaitlyn voiced sadly as she picked up a purple rose, lifted it up to her nose, and breathed in the succulent scent of violet.

Kaitlyn tried to reign in her emotions as she shared the next bit of news. "I met your parents. They are such loving people. Your mom told me that your favorite flowers are roses. Hope you like the bright red ones. The color reminds me of your fiery spirit. 'I also added a few purple roses. They are my favorites," she said while she arranged the flowers around the plaque. "Your family is still suffering much pain over losing you, but now they can start to heal with the closure. I promised myself I'd visit them and offer support as they walk through this process."

"Greg's condition has improved considerably since he was brought home. The weekly therapy sessions are helping him. Due to the severe damage to his head brought on by the fall, the doctors don't know if he'll get his entire memory back, more like seventy-five percent. The family is more than grateful to have that much. He mentions you occasionally, but his memory of that time is foggy. The doctors say that the trauma has erased the incident and maybe anything related to it." Kaitlyn smiled. "I want to believe you exist in a special place in his heart and will always remain there. Sara hasn't said much. As far as she knows, Tatiana was just a plaque on a vehicle."

Kaitlyn paused for a moment to listen to the wind rustling through the trees, singing crows, and dry leaves crunching underneath the feet of the woodland creatures scurrying by. She gave a heavy sigh as she got lost in the sounds of nature.

"Greg has been up to see your great-grandfather Doug, to help out with chores. It took some work, but he finally talked him into seeing a doctor. He is on medication for Alzheimer's. It won't cure it, but it's supposed to slow down the progression and seems to be helping. Sometimes Jason and I tag along to keep Greg company on the drive. Sara has even been up a couple of times. Jason calls him Grandpa Doug." Kaitlyn giggled at the thought. "You'd love it up there. We ride horses, walk the trails, and tell stories around a roaring campfire, underneath a million-star sky show. I want to think you are one of those bright stars, because you've added a spark to my life."

Kaitlyn picked up Gina's ball and tossed it across the meadow and then brought her attention back to Tatiana. "Simon and Steven are supposed to appear in court in a couple months. When the police retrieved your body, they found Steven's ring in your hand, tightly made into a fist. With all the evidence collected, and the discovery of the ring, those two will probably get life in prison. Smart move holding on to it for evidence."

"Tat, I miss you so much. I wish we'd been friends in human form, and you were right here with me now. We'd probably still fight like sisters, you'd push all my buttons and infuriate me to no end, but I'd be able to hug you when we made up," Kaitlyn said with a smirk. "I'm going to miss you." she said in a tearful voice as she stood up. "I should be getting home. Everyone is coming over to my parent's house for dinner, including Doug. I'll tell Jason you said hi and even give him a kiss for you."

As Kaitlyn moved the pattern of the roses one last time, she expressed her wishes. "I only hope that you can hear me. I know you're no longer here and the car is so empty without you, but it would be comforting to know we are still connected. Love you Tat." With that, Kaitlyn turned and left the little hill and headed back.

When she returned to the car, Kaitlyn grabbed a drink from her water bottle and her eyes lit up when the lights on the dash started dancing to the lyrics, *"...Lies the seed, that with the sun's love, in the spring, becomes the rose."*

18) EPILOGUE
FAIRYTALES...

It was after dark when Kaitlyn turned off onto her road. A smile tugged on her lips at the sight of the twinkling lights, guiding her up the hill to her parents'. The magical feeling always made her happy. Tonight, especially, she felt at peace. Kaitlyn was going to miss the pesky spirit. Tatiana was always going to hold a place in Kaitlyn's heart. Because of Tat, she and Jason were brought together and were now blessed with new friends. The night ahead with her family and friends would be a celebration of love and happiness, and healing for many.

When Kaitlyn reached the top of the hill, she was amazed at the turn out of people. There were even cars parked in the overfill parking lot.

This was the work of her mom. Kaitlyn knew how much she enjoyed entertaining and cooking; the more, the better, was her mother's favorite saying. It was a good thing she knew how to cook for an army because it looked like a platoon had been invited to this party. Laughing at where her mind had gone, Kaitlyn climbed out of the car and looked around. "Funny," she said, looking around. "That's odd. Where are all the people," Kaitlyn asked Gina, who was busy exploring and sniffing all the vehicles. "Come on, girl, let's go around back. That must be where the party is."

Kaitlyn opened the gate and found everyone in the grass gathered in a large group, their voices low. The crowd split in two when they noticed her, exposing a red velvet carpet leading to a small stage. Kaitlyn froze as she worked to catch her breath while her heart danced wildly in her chest at the sight of her fairytale prince came to life. Jason, dressed in black dress pants and a crisp white shirt, stood smiling, his eyes pulling her closer. Kaitlyn walked toward her dream man, only it felt more like floating. She wanted to pinch herself to make sure it was real. This kind of thing only happened in a romance movie, she thought.

Jason stood on the stage, his hands sweaty and his legs shaking. He couldn't believe he was about to ask this beautiful woman to marry him.

The question "what if she says no?" crossed his mind. He buried that thought when Kaitlyn stopped, and her loving eyes told him he had nothing to worry about. Taking her hands, he lifted her up on the stage and pulled her close. Then he stepped back, putting twelve inches between them. Jason kneeled on one knee.

Kaitlyn gasped and covered her mouth. Her cheeks glistened with happy tears.

With both her hands resting in his, Jason spoke, "Kaitlyn, you came into my life, a redheaded spitfire that captured my hurting heart. You've challenged me, scared the hell out of me, and tried to protect me. You showed me more kindness and love than I deserved. You helped a sad and bitter man find love again and get his life back. I know you've been hurt, but I promise never to do you wrong." Jason stood; his eyes lost in Kaitlyn's. "So, as I stand here in front of our families and friends, I want to profess my love for you. Would you please do me the honor of being my wife?"

Kaitlyn swallowed, her mouth dry and a lump stuck in her throat. Her body trembled as she faced her prince. "My annoying heartthrob," she giggled nervously, "I didn't want to fall for you, but you pushed your way into my life and finally into my heart. You rescued me more than once but have always respected my boundaries and independence. I've seen your compassion and how much you care for those you love. You're right. Your mom did raise you right. I know you will make an amazing husband and father. I want to raise a family with you and rock away the golden years on our front porch. The answer is a definite YES!" Her hand shook as he slipped the sparkling gem onto her finger. "Beautiful," she said, gazing at the shiny symbol of love on her finger.

"Yes, she is," Jason commented as he whisked her into his arms and kissed her like no one was watching, oblivious to all the catcalls and whistles.

Jason faced the crowd. "She said Yes!" he exclaimed like a giddy schoolboy. His arms wrapped tightly around his fiancé's waist. "I'm never going to let you go," he whispered in her arm.

"And I'll always be here," she whispered back, followed by an affectionate kiss on his cheek. "Let's party!" Kaitlyn yelled out, causing a loud outburst from the crowd. With that, the celebration began, congratulation hugs were handed out, warm toasts were made, and spirits filled the glasses. It was a day she'd never forget. Kaitlyn smiled as she felt a sensation enter her soul and heard a familiar soft voice say, *"Congratulations Sis."*

DON'T MISS:

HISTORIES AND MYSTERIES:
RAZOR SHARP AND DIAMOND CUTS

THE NEXT BOOK IN THE
HISTORIES AND MYSTERIES SERIES

BY LINDA K. RICHISON

She blew into the sleepy little town in the Pacific Northwest on the tail end of a passing storm. New in town, Jewel settled into her new digs in a cozy bachelorette suite on Summer Street. She dusted off her cosmetology license and opened a boutique hair salon & spa on Salem's south side. Her hopes, by pulling up her roots from her Midwest home and planting them firmly in her new surroundings, she'd erase the past and paint a bright new future in the land of knotty pines, hemlocks, and Douglas firs. That was her plan, but she soon learned, nothing is ever as it should be, and very seldom as it could be.

However, 'the best-laid plans...' gave way to the will of a surprise named Gemma. She's a mischievous little spirit with a playful streak on a mission and determined to drag Jewel along. To add to her chaotic daily challenges, Jewel must protect her bruised heart and keep from falling for her debonair and rather sexy shop owner, Vincent.

Sparks fly when Jewel must call on the services of the sexy shop owner, Vincent. Prepare for the fireworks of exploding emotions when Jewel's opinionated and color-outside-of-the-lines lifestyle collide with Vincent's reserved, cautious nature.

Settle into the barber's chair and prepare for a high and tight adventure, like a fading message on an oil-stained postcard, setting them on a journey to untangle this delightful, frosted mystery.

ABOUT THE AUTHOR

Linda K. Richison resides in Salem, Oregon. Linda is a Romance-Fantasy writer who weaves her stories with much care and exciting plots. She is the author of six books including her first series; The Spirit of Love: Heart and Souls, The Spirit of Love: Lost and Found, The Spirit of Love: Spice and Sassy. And her second series; Histories and Mysteries: Charm and Chills, Histories and Mysteries: Red Wine and Black Roses, and Histories and Mysteries: Back Roads and Dangerous Curves. She is always thinking ahead and writing her next book.

She believes in living life to the fullest as she balances writing and spending time with family and friends. She also enjoys outdoor adventures as she loves connecting with nature. Linda is continuing to maintain a healthy lifestyle. An ever-changing goal of keeping physically, mentally, and spiritually fit is always a challenge but is so rewarding as it allows her to keep doing the things she loves.

Linda K. Richison

www.ingramcontent.com/pod-product-compliance
Lightning Source LLC
Chambersburg PA
CBHW071433200726
48294CB00002B/624